STAR WARS

THE MANDALORIAN

SEASON ONE PART TWO

STAR WARS THE MANDALORIAN

SEASON ONE PART TWO

Adapted by

Writer
RODNEY BARNES

Penciler
GEORGES JEANTY

Inker
DEXTER VINES

Colorist
RACHELLE ROSENBERG

Letterer
VC's JOE CARAMAGNA

Cover Art
STEPHANIE HANS (#5),
PATRICK GLEASON & **ALEJANDRO SÁNCHEZ** (#6),
STEVE McNIVEN & **ALEX SINCLAIR** (#7)
and **SARA PICHELLI** & **FEDERICO BLEE** (#8)

Assistant Editor
MIKEY J. BASSO

Associate Editor
DANNY KHAZEM

Editor
MARK PANICCIA

Based on the series created by **JON FAVREAU** and written by
JON FAVREAU, **DAVE FILONI**, **CHRISTOPHER YOST** and **RICK FAMUYIWA**

Collection Editor **JENNIFER GRÜNWALD**
Assistant Editor **DANIEL KIRCHHOFFER**
Assistant Managing Editor **MAIA LOY**
Associate Manager, Talent Relations **LISA MONTALBANO**
VP Production & Special Projects **JEFF YOUNGQUIST**
Book Designer **ADAM DEL RE**
SVP Print, Sales & Marketing **DAVID GABRIEL**
Editor in Chief **C.B. CEBULSKI**

For Lucasfilm:
Senior Editor **ROBERT SIMPSON**
Creative Director **MICHAEL SIGLAIN**
Art Director **TROY ALDERS**
Lucasfilm Story Group **MATT MARTIN**
PABLO HIDALGO
EMILY SHKOUKANI
JAMES WAUGH
Creative Art Manager **PHIL SZOSTAK**

STAR WARS: THE MANDALORIAN - SEASON ONE, PART TWO. Contains material originally published in magazine form as STAR WARS: THE MANDALORIAN (2021) #5-8. First printing 2023. ISBN 978-1-302-93286-2. Published by MARVEL WORLDWIDE, INC., a subsidiary of MARVEL ENTERTAINMENT, LLC. OFFICE OF PUBLICATION: 1290 Avenue of the Americas, New York, NY 10104.

Printed in Canada. KEVIN FEIGE, Chief Creative Officer; DAN BUCKLEY, President, Marvel Entertainment; DAVID BOGART, Associate Publisher & SVP of Talent Affairs; TOM BREVOORT, VP, Executive Editor; NICK LOWE, Executive Editor, VP of Content, Digital Publishing; DAVID GABRIEL, VP of Print & Digital Publishing; SVEN LARSEN, VP of Licensed Publishing; MARK ANNUNZIATO, VP of Planning & Forecasting; JEFF YOUNGQUIST, VP of Production & Special Projects; ALEX MORALES, Director of Publishing Operations; DAN EDINGTON, Director of Editorial Operations; RICKEY PURDIN, Director of Talent Relations; JENNIFER GRÜNWALD, Director of Production & Special Projects; SUSAN CRESPI, Production Manager; STAN LEE, Chairman Emeritus. For information regarding advertising in Marvel Comics or on Marvel.com, please contact Vit DeBellis, Custom Solutions & Integrated Advertising Manager, at vdebellis@marvel.com. For Marvel subscription inquiries, please call 888-511-5480. **Manufactured between 2/17/2023 and 3/21/2023 by SOLISCO PRINTERS, SCOTT, QC, CANADA.**

10 9 8 7 6 5 4 3 2 1

CHAPTER 5: THE GUNSLINGER

After the fall of the Galactic Empire, lawlessness has spread throughout the galaxy.
The Mandalorian travels ever onward, with an unshakable code of honor.
This is the Way. . . .

STAR WARS THE MANDALORIAN

In need of a place to hide with the Child, Mando chose the backwater planet Sorgan. During his time on the planet, he met ex-Rebel soldier Cara Dune as well as a tribe of villagers in desperate need of help against a band of violent raiders. After fighting off the raiders and protecting the village, the Child was still almost taken out by another bounty hunter. Now Mando must continue his journey through space to keep the Child safe....

PEW
PEW
PEW
HAND OVER THE CHILD, MANDO!
I MIGHT LET YOU LIVE!
I CAN BRING YOU IN WARM...OR I CAN BRING YOU IN COLD.

VROOOOOOOOM
THAT'S MY LINE.
BOOOM

THIS IS MOS EISLEY TOWER. WE ARE TRACKING YOU. HEAD FOR BAY THREE-FIVE, OVER.
COPY THAT. LOCKED IN FOR THREE-FIVE.

PEW!
HEY!

YOU DAMAGE ONE OF MY DROIDS, YOU'LL PAY FOR IT!
JUST KEEP THEM AWAY FROM MY SHIP.
YOU THINK THAT'S A GOOD IDEA? GOT A LOT OF CARBON SCORIN' BUILDING UP TOP. IF I DIDN'T KNOW BETTER, I'D THINK YOU WERE IN A SHOOT-OUT.
YOU GOT A FUEL LEAK. THIS IS A MESS! HOW DID YOU EVEN LAND?
I'VE GOT FIVE HUNDRED IMPERIAL CREDITS.
WELL, WHAT DO YOU GUYS THINK?
THAT SHOULD AT LEAST COVER THE HANGAR.
I'LL GET YOU YOUR MONEY.
HMM. I'VE HEARD THAT BEFORE.
JUST REMEMBER--
YEAH, NO DROIDS. I HEARD YA. YOU DON'T HAVE TO SAY IT TWICE.

I'M IN. AND I'M GONNA RAISE YOU...THREE BOLTS AND A MOTIVATOR.
RRRRRGGGGKKKTT
I'D STAY IN THAT SHIP IF I WERE YOU!
WHAT?
DID THAT BOUNTY HUNTER LEAVE YOU ALL ALONE IN THAT BIG, NASTY SHIP?
NOW, HERE'S THE PLAN. I AM GOING TO LOOK AFTER YOU UNTIL THE MANDALORIAN GETS BACK, AND THEN I'M GOING TO CHARGE HIM EXTRA FOR WATCHING YOU.

HEY, DROID, I'M A HUNTER. I'M LOOKING FOR SOME WORK.
UNFORTUNATELY, THE BOUNTY GUILD NO LONGER OPERATES FROM TATOOINE.
I'M NOT LOOKING FOR GUILD WORK.
I AM AFRAID THAT DOES NOT IMPROVE YOUR SITUATION, AT LEAST BY MY CALCULATION.
THINK AGAIN, TIN CAN.
IF YOU'RE LOOKING FOR WORK, HAVE A SEAT, MY FRIEND. NAME'S TORO, TORO CALICAN. COME ON, RELAX.
PICKED UP THIS BOUNTY PUCK BEFORE I LEFT THE MID RIM. FENNEC SHAND, AN ASSASSIN. HEARD SHE'S BEEN ON THE RUN EVER SINCE THE NEW REPUBLIC PUT ALL HER EMPLOYERS IN LOCKDOWN.
I KNOW THE NAME.

I FOLLOWED THIS TRACKING FOB HERE. NOW THE POSITIONAL DATA SUGGESTS SHE'S HEADED OUT BEYOND THE DUNE SEA. SHOULD BE AN EASY JOB.
WELL, GOOD LUCK WITH THAT.
I THOUGHT YOU NEEDED WORK?
HOW LONG YOU BEEN WITH THE GUILD?
LONG ENOUGH.
CLEARLY NOT. FENNEC SHAND IS AN ELITE MERCENARY. SHE MADE HER NAME KILLING FOR ALL THE TOP CRIME SYNDICATES, INCLUDING THE HUTTS. IF YOU GO AFTER HER, YOU WON'T MAKE IT PAST SUNRISE.
THIS IS MY FIRST JOB. YOU CAN KEEP THE MONEY, ALL OF IT. I JUST NEED THIS JOB TO GET INTO THE GUILD. I CAN'T DO IT ALONE.
MEET ME AT HANGAR THREE-FIVE IN HALF AN HOUR. BRING TWO SPEEDER BIKES, AND GIVE ME THE TRACKING FOB.

DON'T WORRY, GOT IT ALL MEMORIZED.
HALF AN HOUR.
LOOKS LIKE YOU'RE STUCK WITH ME NOW, PARTNER!
WHERE IS HE?!
AGH! I'M AWAKE! I'M AWAKE!
YOU WOKE IT UP! DO YOU HAVE ANY IDEA HOW LONG IT TOOK ME TO GET IT TO *SLEEP?*
GIVE HIM TO ME.

YOU CAN'T JUST LEAVE A CHILD ALL ALONE LIKE THAT. YOU HAVE AN AWFUL LOT TO LEARN ABOUT RAISIN' A YOUNG ONE.
ANYWAY, I STARTED THE REPAIR ON THE FUEL LEAK. HAD A COUPLE SETBACKS I WANT TO TALK TO YOU ABOUT.
I DIDN'T USE ANY DROIDS--AS REQUESTED--SO IT TOOK ME A LOT LONGER THAN I EXPECTED. BUT I FIGURED YOU WERE GOOD FOR THE MONEY SINCE YOU HAVE AN EXTRA MOUTH TO FEED.
THANK YOU.
GUESS I WAS RIGHT! YOU GOT A JOB, DIDN'T YOU? YOU KNOW, IT'S COSTING ME A LOT OF MONEY TO KEEP THESE DROIDS EVEN POWERED UP.
HEY, MANDO, WHAT DO YOU THINK? NOT TOO SHABBY, HUH?

VZZRREWWW
WHAT'S GOING ON?
LOOK. UP AHEAD.
TUSKEN RAIDERS. I HEARD THE LOCALS TALKING ABOUT THIS FILTH.
TUSKENS THINK THEY'RE THE LOCALS. EVERYONE ELSE IS JUST TRESPASSING.
WELL, WHATEVER THEY CALL THEMSELVES, THEY'D BEST KEEP THEIR DISTANCE.
YEAH? WHY DON'T YOU TELL THEM YOURSELF?

RELAX.
WHAT ARE YOU DOING?
NEGOTIATING.
WHAT'S GOING ON?
WE NEED PASSAGE ACROSS THEIR LAND.
LET ME SEE THE BINOCS.
WHY?
HEY! THOSE WERE BRAND NEW!
YEAH? THEY WERE.

GET DOWN!
ALL RIGHT, TELL ME WHAT YOU SEE.
DEWBACK. LOOKS LIKE THE RIDER IS STILL ATTACHED. IS THAT HER? IS THAT THE TARGET?
I DON'T KNOW. I'LL GO. YOU COVER ME.
IS IT HER? IS SHE DEAD?
IT'S ANOTHER BOUNTY HUNTER.
I HOPE YOU DON'T PLAN ON KEEPING ALL THAT STUFF FOR YOURSELF. CAN I AT LEAST HAVE THAT BLASTER?

GET DOWN!
MANDO!
500
WHAT HAPPENED?
SNIPER BOLT. ONLY AN MK-MODIFIED *RIFLE* COULD MAKE THAT SHOT.
ARE YOU ALL RIGHT?
YEAH. HIT ME IN THE BESKAR, AND AT THAT RANGE, BESKAR HELD UP.
WAIT, I DON'T WEAR ANY BESKAR.
NOPE.

YOU SEE WHERE THAT SHOT CAME FROM?
YEAH, IT CAME FROM THAT RIDGE.
OKAY, WE'RE GONNA WAIT UNTIL DARK.
WELL, WHAT IF SHE ESCAPES?
SHE'S GOT THE HIGH GROUND. SHE'LL WAIT FOR US TO MAKE THE FIRST MOVE. I'M GONNA REST. YOU TAKE THE FIRST WATCH. STAY LOW!
ALL RIGHT, SUNS ARE DOWN. TIME TO RIDE, MANDO.
LOOK AT YOU, ASLEEP ON THE JOB, OLD MAN.

YOU DONE?
YEAH. I WAS JUST, YOU KNOW, WAKING YOU UP. COME ON.
GET ON YOUR BIKE. RIDE AS FAST AS YOU CAN TOWARD THOSE ROCKS.
THAT'S YOUR PLAN? SHE'LL SNIPE US RIGHT OFF THE BIKES.
IT'S A FLASH CHARGE. WE ALTERNATE SHOTS, IT'LL BLIND ANY SCOPE TEMPORARILY. COMBINE THAT WITH OUR SPEED, AND WE GOT A CHANCE.
A CHANCE?
HEY, YOU WANTED THIS.

VZZRREWWWW
PEWINNNG

PSHEW
NOW!
PEWWWWSSH
PFBOOM

NOT SO FAST, FENNEC.
PING

CRACK
UNH!
HUAH!
AAAHH!
NICE DISTRACTION.

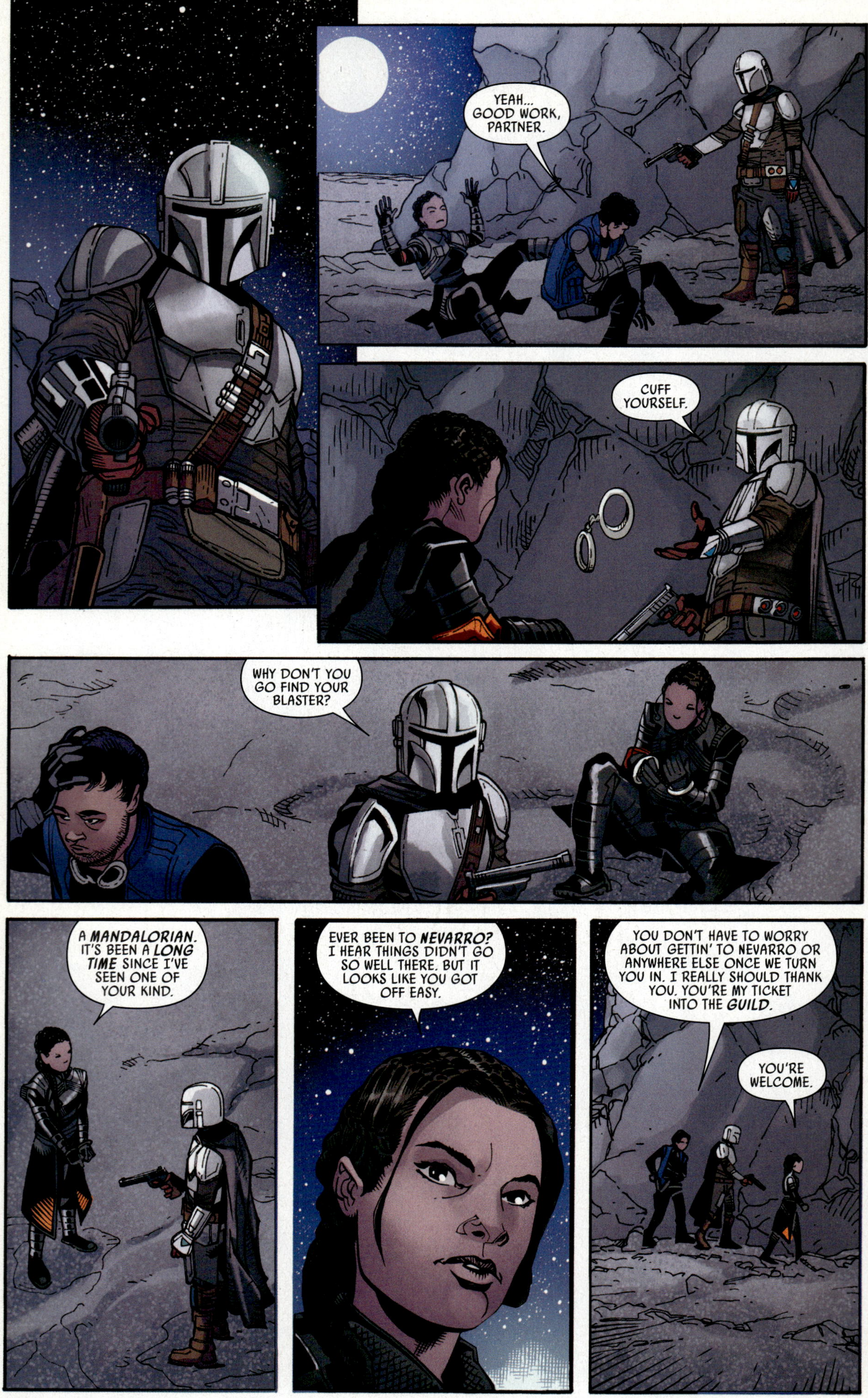
YEAH... GOOD WORK, PARTNER.
CUFF YOURSELF.
WHY DON'T YOU GO FIND YOUR BLASTER?
A MANDALORIAN. IT'S BEEN A LONG TIME SINCE I'VE SEEN ONE OF YOUR KIND.
EVER BEEN TO NEVARRO? I HEAR THINGS DIDN'T GO SO WELL THERE. BUT IT LOOKS LIKE YOU GOT OFF EASY.
YOU DON'T HAVE TO WORRY ABOUT GETTIN' TO NEVARRO OR ANYWHERE ELSE ONCE WE TURN YOU IN. I REALLY SHOULD THANK YOU. YOU'RE MY TICKET INTO THE GUILD.
YOU'RE WELCOME.

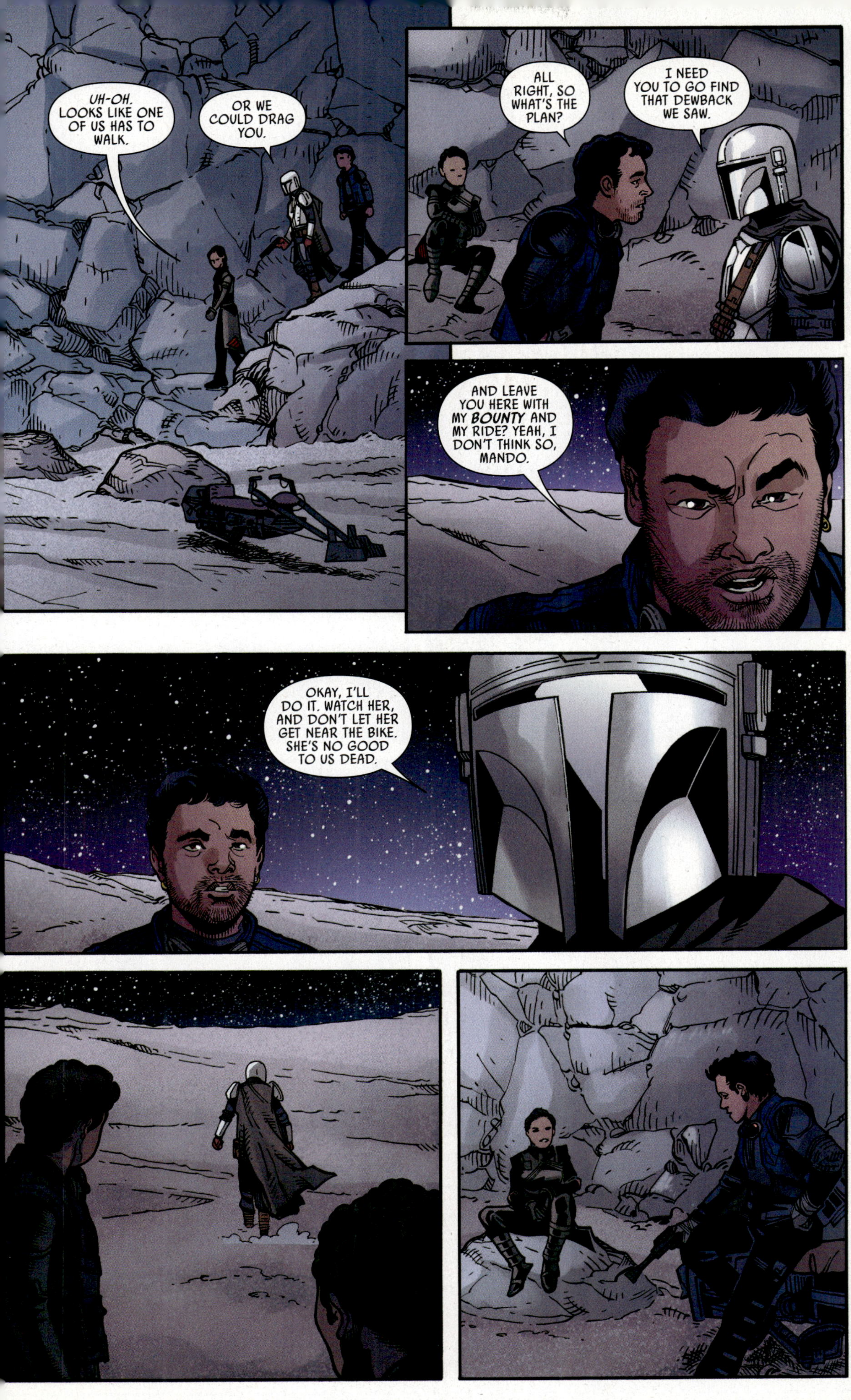
UH-OH. LOOKS LIKE ONE OF US HAS TO WALK.
OR WE COULD DRAG YOU.
ALL RIGHT, SO WHAT'S THE PLAN?
I NEED YOU TO GO FIND THAT DEWBACK WE SAW.
AND LEAVE YOU HERE WITH MY *BOUNTY* AND MY RIDE? YEAH, I DON'T THINK SO, MANDO.
OKAY, I'LL DO IT. WATCH HER, AND DON'T LET HER GET NEAR THE BIKE. SHE'S NO GOOD TO US DEAD.

OH, LOOK, THE SUNS ARE COMING UP.
QUIET.
LOOK, THERE'S STILL TIME TO MAKE MY RENDEZVOUS IN MOS ESPA. TAKE ME TO IT AND I CAN PAY YOU DOUBLE THE PRICE ON MY HEAD.
I DON'T CARE ABOUT THE MONEY.
OH, SO THE MANDALORIAN KEEPS ALL THE MONEY FOR HIMSELF.
ONLY BECAUSE I LET HIM.
DOESN'T SEEM THAT WAY. SEEMS LIKE HE'S CALLING ALL THE SHOTS.
SHOWS WHAT YOU KNOW. I HIRED MANDO--THIS IS *MY* JOB. BRINGING YOU IN WILL MAKE ME A FULL MEMBER OF THE BOUNTY HUNTERS GUILD.
YOU ALREADY HAVE SOMETHING THE GUILD VALUES FAR MORE THAN ME. YOU JUST DON'T SEE IT.
WHAT?
THE MANDALORIAN. HIS ARMOR ALONE'S WORTH MORE THAN MY BOUNTY.
I ALREADY TOLD YOU, I DON'T CARE ABOUT THE MONEY.
THEN THINK WHAT IT WOULD DO FOR YOUR REPUTATION.

A MANDALORIAN SHOT UP THE GUILD ON NEVARRO, TOOK SOME HIGH-VALUE TARGET AND WENT ROGUE.
THAT MANDALORIAN?
LIKE I SAID, YOU DON'T SEE MANY.
YOU BRING THE GUILD THAT TRAITOR, AND THEY'LL WELCOME YOU WITH OPEN ARMS. YOUR NAME WILL BE LEGENDARY.
HOW CAN WE BE SURE HE'S THE ONE?
WORD IS, HE STILL HAS THE TARGET WITH HIM.
SOME SAY IT'S A CHILD.
LOOK, IF YOU'RE AFRAID TO TAKE HIM ON, FEAR NOT. I CAN HELP YOU WITH THAT.
TAKE SOME ADVICE, KID. YOU WANNA BE A BOUNTY HUNTER? MAKE THE BEST DEAL FOR YOURSELF... AND SURVIVE.

PEW
THAT'S GOOD ADVICE. BUT IF I TOOK THOSE BINDERS OFF YOU, I'D BE A DEAD MAN.
AND IF THE MANDALORIAN'S WORTH MORE THAN YOU ARE, WELL...WHO WOULDN'T WANT TO BE A LEGEND?
THANKS FOR THE TIP.

SNNOORTT
TOOK YOU LONG ENOUGH, MANDO.

LOOKS LIKE I'M CALLING THE SHOTS NOW, HUH, PARTNER?
DROP YOUR BLASTER AND RAISE 'EM.
CUFF HIM.
YOU'RE A GUILD TRAITOR, MANDO. AND I'M WILLING TO BET THAT THIS HERE IS THE TARGET YOU HELPED ESCAPE.
YOU'RE SMARTER THAN YOU LOOK.
BRINGING YOU IN WON'T JUST MAKE ME A MEMBER OF THE GUILD...
...IT'LL MAKE ME LEGENDARY.

PEW
PEW
PEW
THERE YOU ARE! ARE YOU HIDING FROM US? HUH? LOOK AT YOU!
WHERE IS IT?!

THAT WAS REALLY LOUD FOR YOUR BIG OLD EARS, WASN'T IT?
SO, I TAKE IT YOU DIDN'T GET PAID?
THAT COVER ME?
YEAH. YEAH, THIS IS GONNA COVER YOU.
ALL RIGHT, PIT DROIDS! LET'S DRAG THIS *OUTTA* HERE!

CHAPTER 6: THE PRISONER

MANDO! IS THAT YOU UNDER THAT BUCKET?
RAN.
DIDN'T KNOW IF I'D EVER SEE YOU IN THESE PARTS AGAIN. GOOD TO SEE YOU.
I WAS A LITTLE SURPRISED WHEN YOU REACHED OUT TO ME. 'CAUSE I... I HEAR THINGS.
LIKE MAYBE THINGS BETWEEN YOU AND THE GUILD AREN'T WORKIN' OUT?
I'LL BE FINE.
WELL, YOU KNOW THE POLICY. NO QUESTIONS. AND YOU'RE WELCOME BACK HERE ANYTIME.

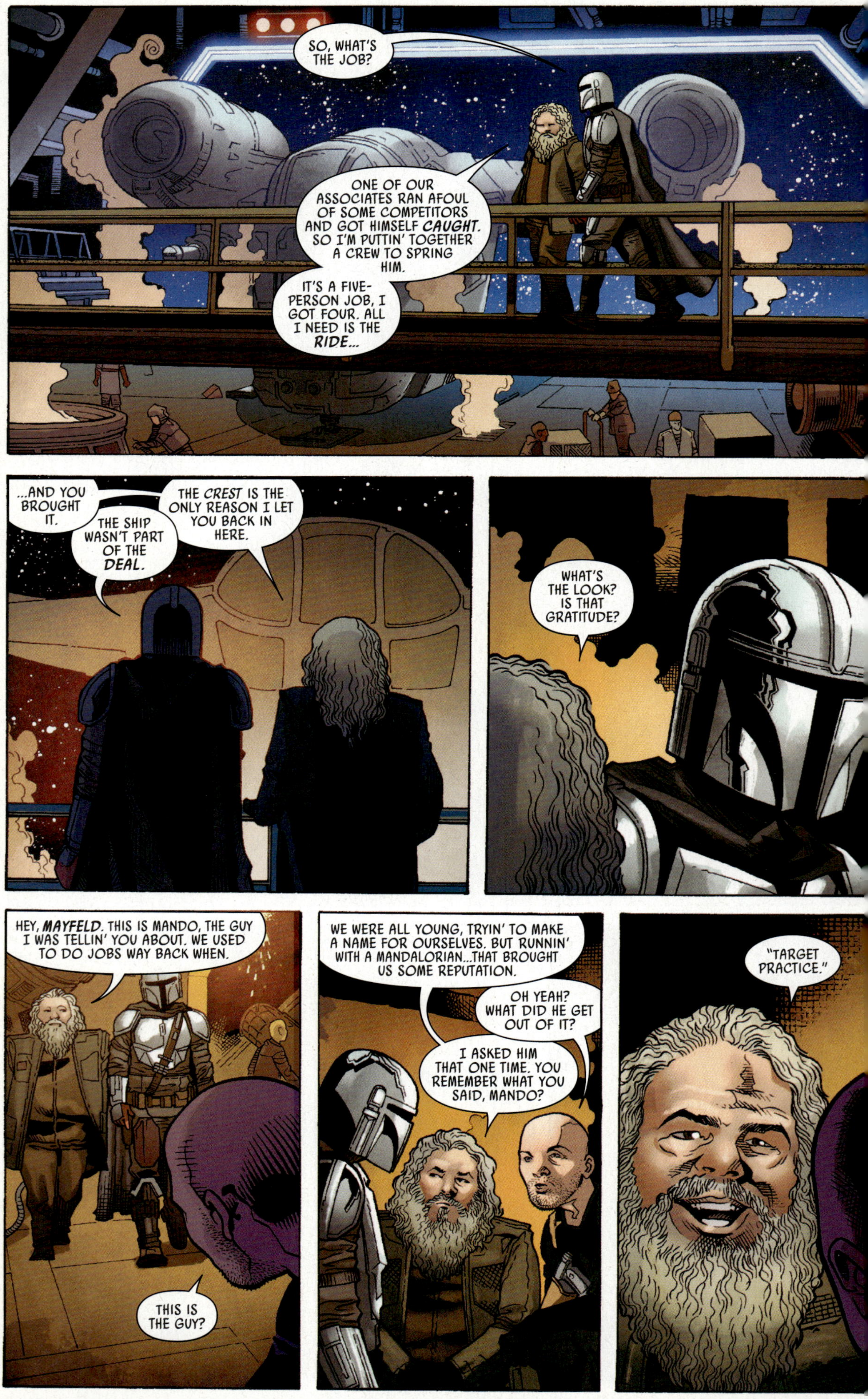
SO, WHAT'S THE JOB?
ONE OF OUR ASSOCIATES RAN AFOUL OF SOME COMPETITORS AND GOT HIMSELF *CAUGHT*. SO I'M PUTTIN' TOGETHER A CREW TO SPRING HIM.
IT'S A FIVE-PERSON JOB, I GOT FOUR. ALL I NEED IS THE *RIDE*...
...AND YOU BROUGHT IT.
THE SHIP WASN'T PART OF THE *DEAL*.
THE *CREST* IS THE ONLY REASON I LET YOU BACK IN HERE.
WHAT'S THE LOOK? IS THAT GRATITUDE?
HEY, *MAYFELD*. THIS IS MANDO, THE GUY I WAS TELLIN' YOU ABOUT. WE USED TO DO JOBS WAY BACK WHEN.
THIS IS THE GUY?
WE WERE ALL YOUNG, TRYIN' TO MAKE A NAME FOR OURSELVES. BUT RUNNIN' WITH A MANDALORIAN...THAT BROUGHT US SOME REPUTATION.
OH YEAH? WHAT DID HE GET OUT OF IT?
I ASKED HIM THAT ONE TIME. YOU REMEMBER WHAT YOU SAID, MANDO?
"TARGET PRACTICE."

I DON'T GO OUT ANYMORE, SO MAYFELD'S GONNA RUN POINT ON THIS JOB. IF HE SAYS IT, IT'S LIKE IT'S COMIN' FROM ME. YOU GOOD WITH THAT?
YOU TELL ME.
YOU HAVEN'T CHANGED ONE BIT. MAYFELD'S ONE OF THE BEST *TRIGGERMEN* I'VE EVER SEEN. FORMER IMPERIAL SHARPSHOOTER.
THAT'S NOT SAYING MUCH.
I WASN'T A STORMTROOPER, WISEASS!
DON'T TAKE LONG, DOES IT?

RAZOR CREST? I CAN'T BELIEVE THAT THING CAN FLY. LOOKS LIKE A CANTO BIGHT SLOT MACHINE.
THE GOOD- LOOKIN' FELLOW THERE WITH THE HORNS, THAT'S BURG. THIS MAY SURPRISE YOU, BUT HE'S OUR MUSCLE.
SO, THIS IS A MANDALORIAN. I THOUGHT THEY'D BE BIGGER.
DROID'S NAME IS ZERO.
I THOUGHT YOU SAID YOU HAD FOUR.
HE DOES.
HELLO, MANDO.
XI'AN.
TELL ME WHY I SHOULDN'T CUT YOU DOWN WHERE YOU STAND?

NICE TO SEE YOU TOO.
THIS IS SHINY. YOU WEAR IT WELL.
DO WE NEED TO LEAVE THE ROOM OR SOMETHING?
XI'AN'S BEEN A LITTLE HEARTBROKEN SINCE MANDO LEFT OUR GROUP.
AWWW, YOU GONNA BE OKAY, SWEETHEART?
I'M ALL BUSINESS NOW.
LEARNED FROM THE BEST.
TINY.

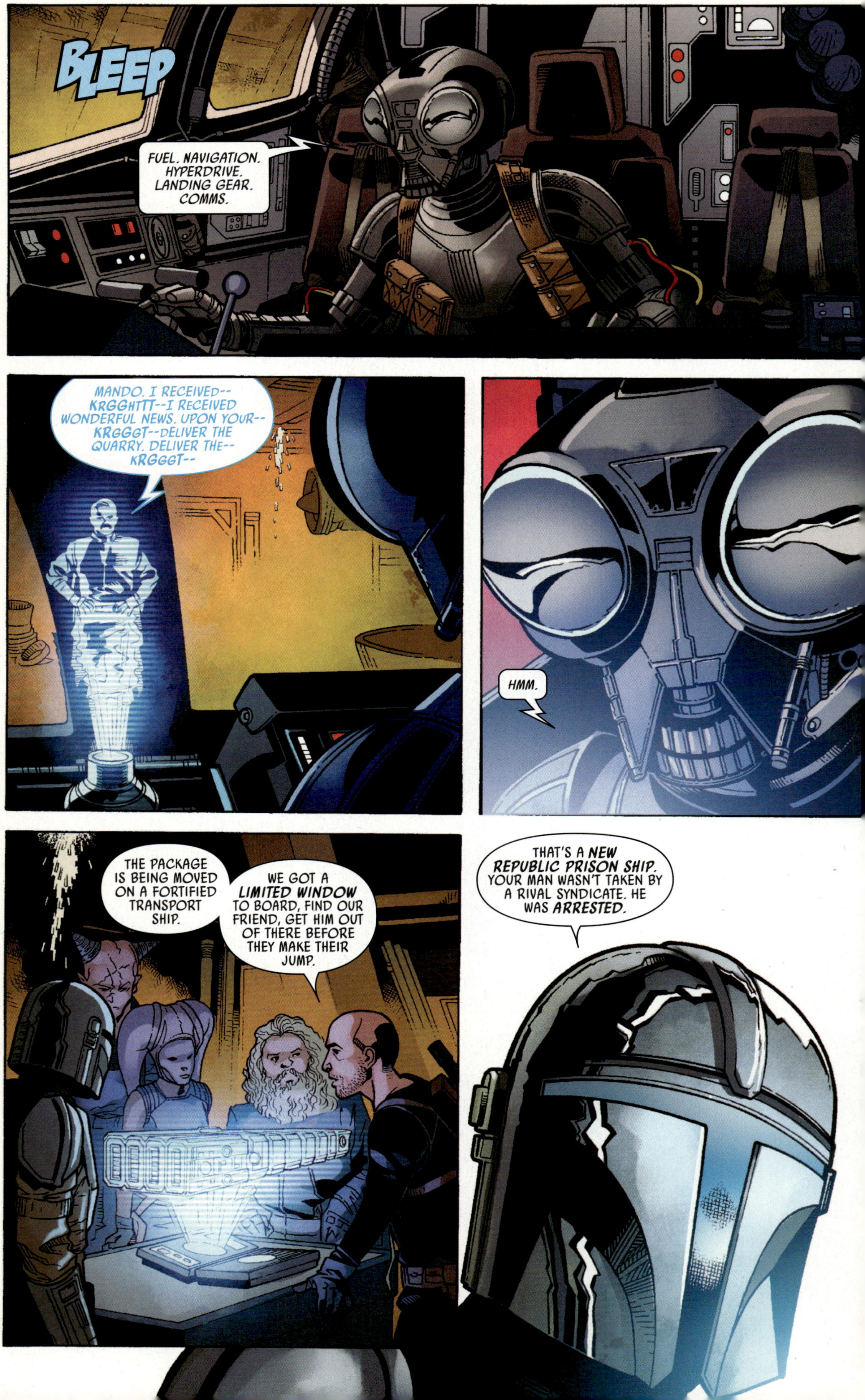
BLEEP
FUEL. NAVIGATION. HYPERDRIVE. LANDING GEAR. COMMS.
MANDO. I RECEIVED-- KRGGHTTT--I RECEIVED WONDERFUL NEWS. UPON YOUR-- KRGGGT--DELIVER THE QUARRY. DELIVER THE-- KRGGGT--
HMM.
THE PACKAGE IS BEING MOVED ON A FORTIFIED TRANSPORT SHIP.
WE GOT A LIMITED WINDOW TO BOARD, FIND OUR FRIEND, GET HIM OUT OF THERE BEFORE THEY MAKE THEIR JUMP.
THAT'S A NEW REPUBLIC PRISON SHIP. YOUR MAN WASN'T TAKEN BY A RIVAL SYNDICATE. HE WAS ARRESTED.

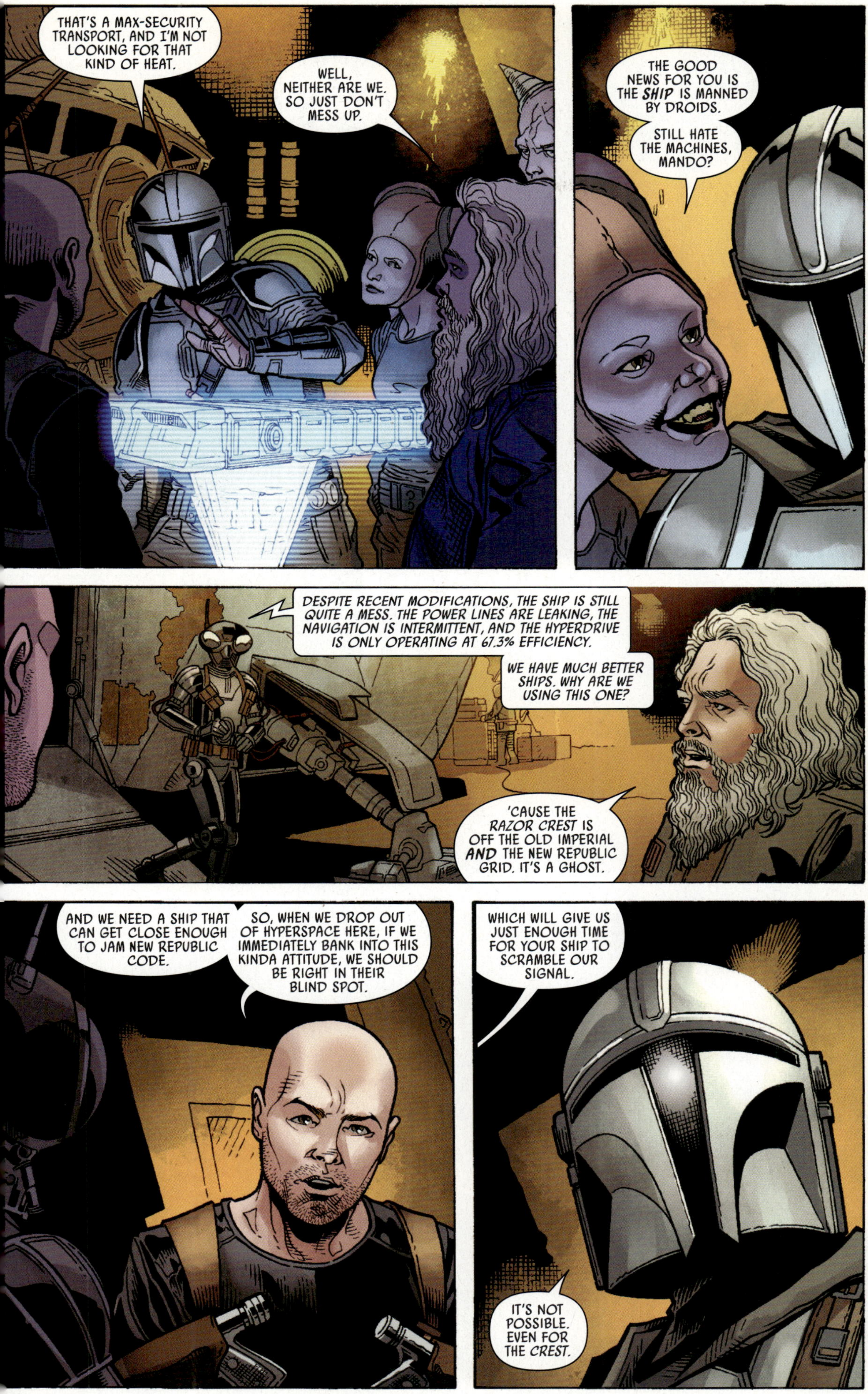
THAT'S A MAX-SECURITY TRANSPORT, AND I'M NOT LOOKING FOR THAT KIND OF HEAT.
WELL, NEITHER ARE WE. SO JUST DON'T MESS UP.
THE GOOD NEWS FOR YOU IS THE *SHIP* IS MANNED BY DROIDS.
STILL HATE THE MACHINES, MANDO?
DESPITE RECENT MODIFICATIONS, THE SHIP IS STILL QUITE A MESS. THE POWER LINES ARE LEAKING, THE NAVIGATION IS INTERMITTENT, AND THE HYPERDRIVE IS ONLY OPERATING AT 67.3% EFFICIENCY.
WE HAVE MUCH BETTER SHIPS. WHY ARE WE USING THIS ONE?
'CAUSE THE *RAZOR CREST* IS OFF THE OLD IMPERIAL ***AND*** THE NEW REPUBLIC GRID. IT'S A GHOST.
AND WE NEED A SHIP THAT CAN GET CLOSE ENOUGH TO JAM NEW REPUBLIC CODE.
SO, WHEN WE DROP OUT OF HYPERSPACE HERE, IF WE IMMEDIATELY BANK INTO THIS KINDA ATTITUDE, WE SHOULD BE RIGHT IN THEIR BLIND SPOT.
WHICH WILL GIVE US JUST ENOUGH TIME FOR YOUR SHIP TO SCRAMBLE OUR SIGNAL.
IT'S NOT POSSIBLE. EVEN FOR THE *CREST*.

THAT'S WHY HE'S FLYING.
WE NEED YOU ON THE TRIGGER. NOT ON THE WHEEL.
DON'T WORRY, MANDALORIAN. MY RESPONSE TIME IS QUICKER THAN ORGANICS. AND I'M SMARTER TOO.
FORGIVE THE PROGRAMMING. HE'S A LITTLE ROUGH AROUND THE EDGES. BUT HE IS THE BEST.
HOW CAN YOU TRUST IT?
YOU KNOW ME, MANDO. I DON'T TRUST ANYBODY.
JUST LIKE THE GOOD OLD DAYS, MANDO. HUH?

CALCULATIONS COMPLETE. JUMPING TO HYPERSPACE... NOW.
FEEL FREE TO JOIN THE OTHERS. I WILL HANDLE IT FROM HERE.
DEET DEET DEET
CLANK!

SOMEONE TELL ME WHY WE EVEN NEED A MANDALORIAN.
WELL, *APPARENTLY,* THEY'RE THE GREATEST WARRIORS IN THE GALAXY.
THEN WHY ARE THEY ALL *DEAD?*
YOU FLEW WITH HIM, XI'AN. IS HE AS GOOD AS THEY SAY?
ASK HIM ABOUT THE JOB ON *ALZOC III.*
I DID WHAT I HAD TO.
OH, BUT YOU *LIKED* IT.
HE NEVER TAKES OFF THE HELMET?
"THIS IS THE WAY."
I WONDER WHAT YOU LOOK LIKE UNDER THERE. MAYBE HE'S A *GUNGAN.*

IS THAT WHY "YOUSA DON'T WANNA SHOW YOUR FACE"?
YOU EVER SEEN HIS FACE?
A LADY... NEVER TELLS.
COME ON, MANDO. WE ALL GOTTA TRUST EACH OTHER HERE. LIFT THE HELMET UP.
LET US ALL SEE YOUR EYES.
BLOOP BLOOP!

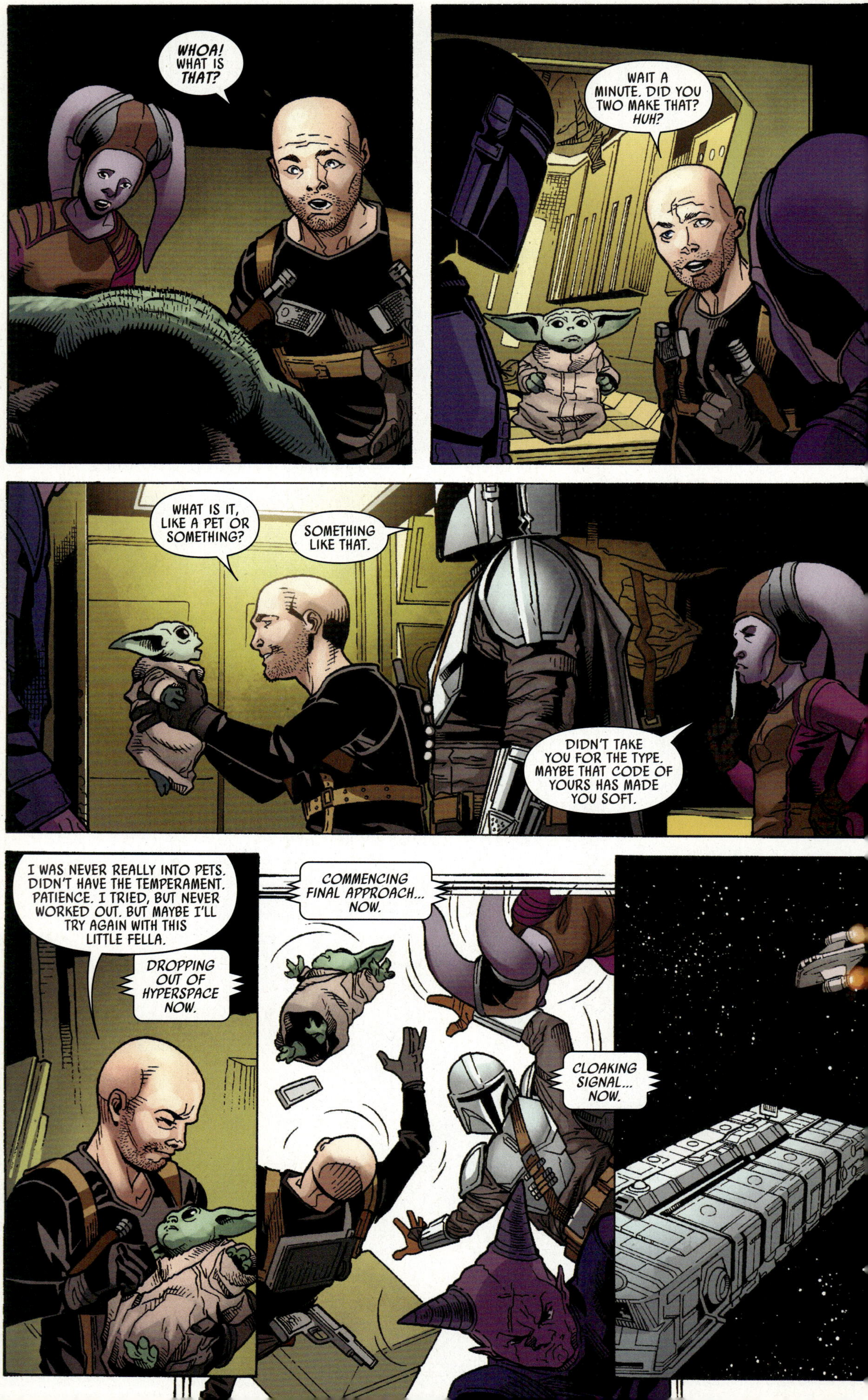
WHOA! WHAT IS THAT?
WAIT A MINUTE. DID YOU TWO MAKE THAT? HUH?
WHAT IS IT, LIKE A PET OR SOMETHING?
SOMETHING LIKE THAT.
DIDN'T TAKE YOU FOR THE TYPE. MAYBE THAT CODE OF YOURS HAS MADE YOU SOFT.
I WAS NEVER REALLY INTO PETS. DIDN'T HAVE THE TEMPERAMENT. PATIENCE. I TRIED, BUT NEVER WORKED OUT. BUT MAYBE I'LL TRY AGAIN WITH THIS LITTLE FELLA.
DROPPING OUT OF HYPERSPACE NOW.
COMMENCING FINAL APPROACH... NOW.
CLOAKING SIGNAL... NOW.

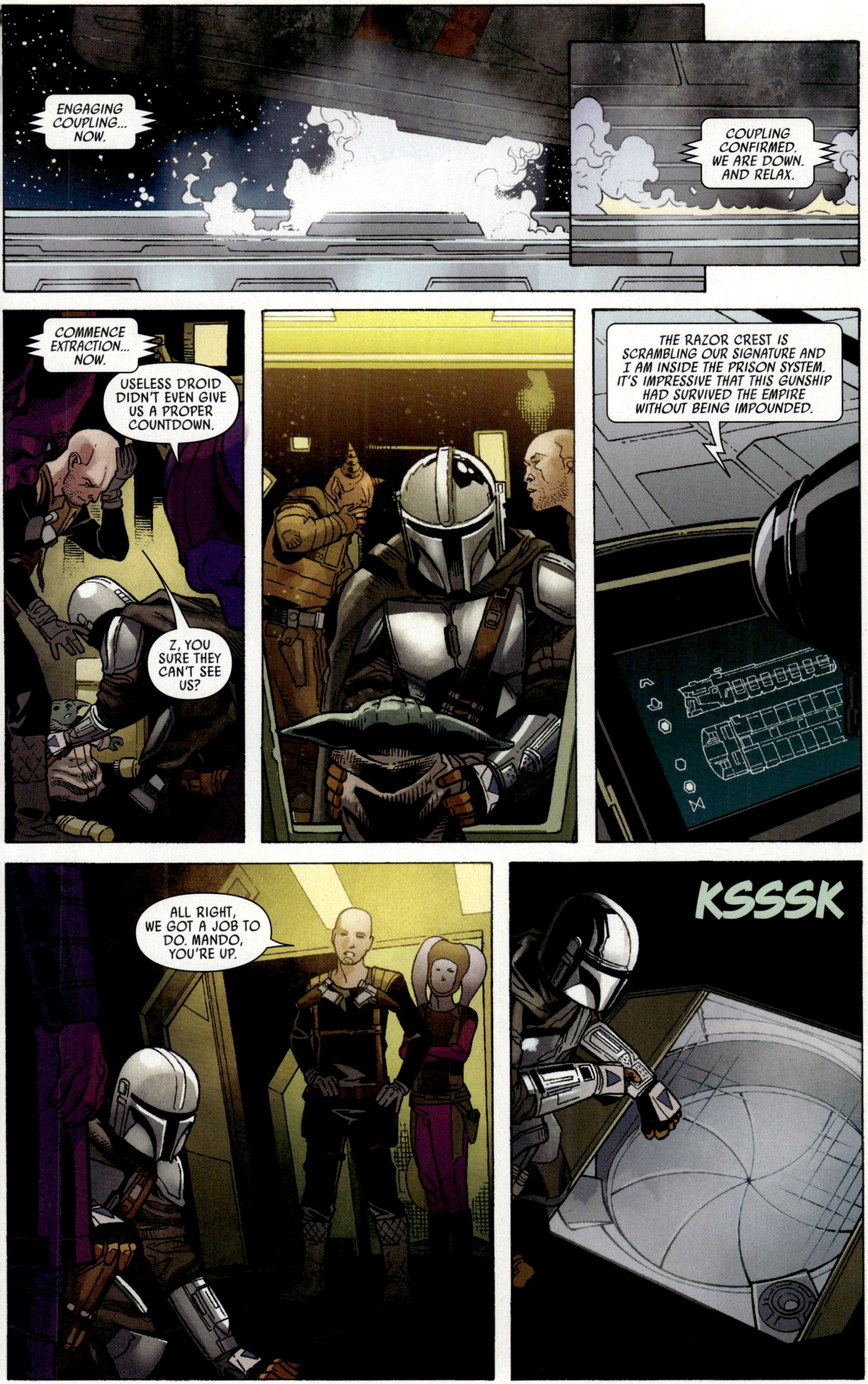
ENGAGING COUPLING... NOW.
COUPLING CONFIRMED. WE ARE DOWN. AND RELAX.
COMMENCE EXTRACTION... NOW.
USELESS DROID DIDN'T EVEN GIVE US A PROPER COUNTDOWN.
Z, YOU SURE THEY CAN'T SEE US?
THE RAZOR CREST IS SCRAMBLING OUR SIGNATURE AND I AM INSIDE THE PRISON SYSTEM. IT'S IMPRESSIVE THAT THIS GUNSHIP HAD SURVIVED THE EMPIRE WITHOUT BEING IMPOUNDED.
ALL RIGHT, WE GOT A JOB TO DO. MANDO, YOU'RE UP.
KSSSK

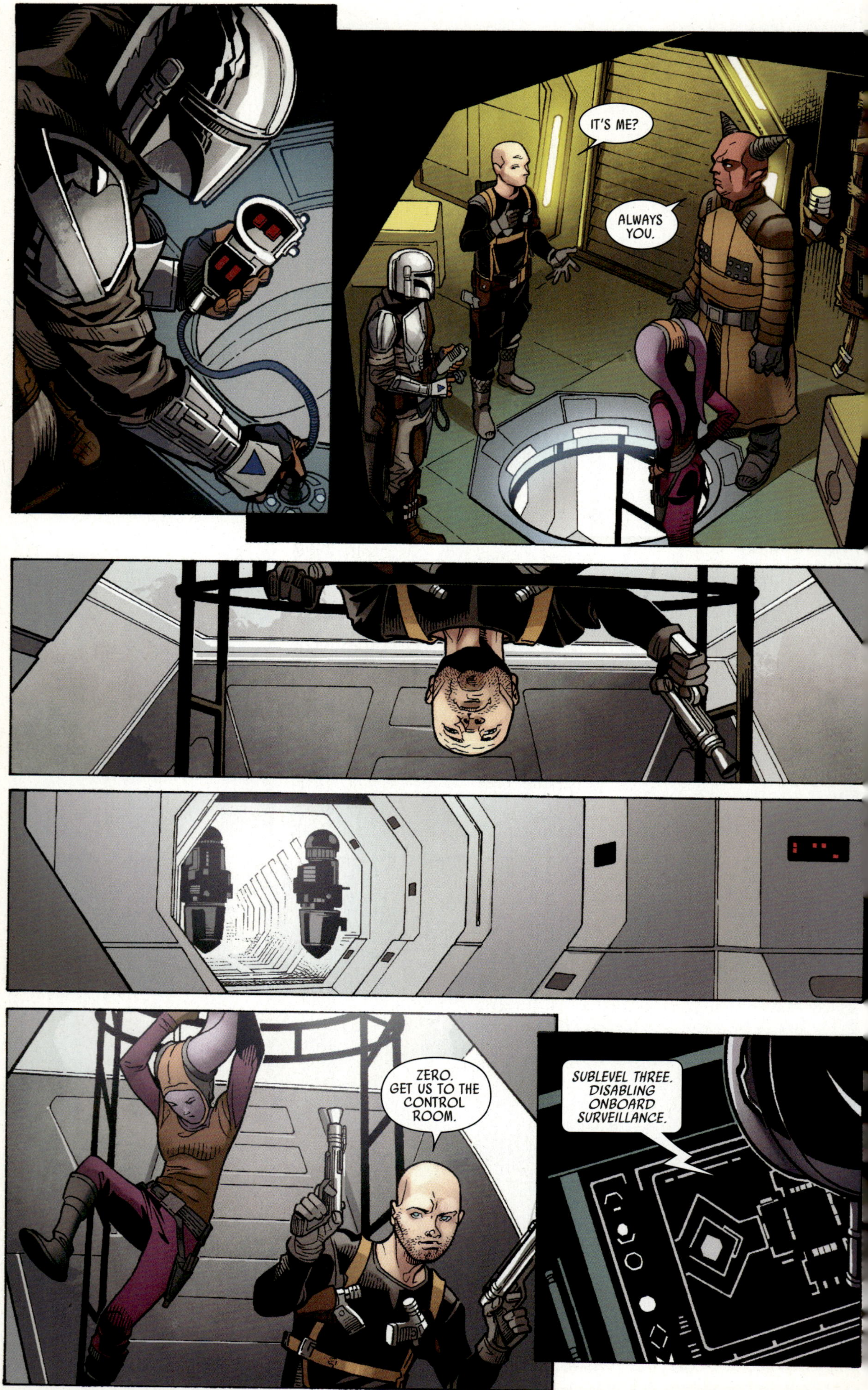
IT'S ME?
ALWAYS YOU.
ZERO. GET US TO THE CONTROL ROOM.
SUBLEVEL THREE. DISABLING ONBOARD SURVEILLANCE.

ALL RIGHT, WE'RE ON THE CLOCK. THE SECOND WE ENGAGE THOSE DROIDS, THEY'RE GONNA BE ALL OVER US.
I KNOW THE DRILL.
BIO TRACKERS ACTIVATED. I'VE GOT EYES.
ALL RIGHT, LET'S GO.
I DON'T LIKE THIS.
YOU ALWAYS WERE *PARANOID*.
IS THAT TRUE, MANDO? WERE YOU ALWAYS PARANOID?

ARGHHHHHEIEIIIIEGGG!
=HISS!=
APPROACHING CONTROL ROOM. MAKE A LEFT AT THE NEXT JUNCTURE.
BLEEP BLEEP BLOOP
WHAT? IT'S JUST A LITTLE MOUSEY.
COME HERE, MOUSEY. COME HERE.
BURG...

BURG! WHAT ARE YOU DOIN'?!
PEW
GRSSHBOOM
INTRUDER ALERT. OPEN FIRE.
MANDO, LET'S GO! YOU'RE SUPPOSED TO BE SOMETHING SPE--
PEW PEW
I KNEW IT. I KNEW IT!

PEW PEW
DINK
DINK
PEWSSH
FFFFRRSSH
PEW

MAKE SURE YOU CLEAN UP YOUR MESS.
YOUR PRESENCE HAS BEEN DETECTED. REDIRECTING SECURITY ALERT AWAY FROM YOUR POSITION.
Z, OPEN THE DOOR!
BUT I'M DETECTING AN ORGANIC SIGNATURE--
JUST OPEN THE DOOR!
STOP RIGHT THERE! PUT DOWN YOUR BLASTERS RIGHT NOW!
NICE SHOES. MATCHES HIS BELT.
PUT DOWN YOUR BLASTERS!
THERE WERE ONLY SUPPOSED TO BE DROIDS ON THIS SHIP.
LET'S SEE HERE, CELL 221.
NOW FOR OUR WELL-DRESSED FRIEND.
WHOA, WHOA, WHOA, WHOA. HEY, EASY...EASY, EGGHEAD. PUT THAT DOWN. COME ON.

PUT IT DOWN NOW!
EASY. NOBODY HAS TO GET HURT HERE. JUST CALM DOWN.
WHAT IS THAT THING?
IT'S A TRACKING BEACON.
HE PRESSES THAT THING, WE'RE ALL DONE. A NEW REPUBLIC ATTACK TEAM WILL HONE IN ON THAT SIGNAL AND BLOW US ALL TO HELL.
ARE YOU SERIOUS? YOU DIDN'T THINK WE NEEDED TO KNOW THAT TINY, LITTLE DETAIL?
I DIDN'T THINK WE'D GET TO THIS POINT!
YET HERE WE ARE.
ARE YOU QUESTIONING MY MANAGERIAL STYLE, XI'AN?
NO, SIR!
HEY. LISTEN TO ME. LOOK.
ARE YOU CRAZY?
PUT IT DOWN.

WHAT'S YOUR NAME?
IT'S DAVAN.
DAVAN. WE'RE NOT HERE FOR YOU. WE'RE HERE FOR A PRISONER. IF YOU LET US GO ABOUT OUR JOB, YOU CAN WALK AWAY WITH YOUR LIFE.
NO, HE WON'T!
YOU REALIZE WHAT YOU'RE GONNA BRING DOWN ON US?
YOU THINK I CARE ABOUT THAT?
WE'RE NOT KILLING ANYBODY. UNDERSTAND?
GET THAT BLASTER OUT OF MY FACE, MANDO.
I CAN'T DO THAT.
GET THAT BLASTER OUT OF MY FACE, MANDO!
DON'T.
FWIP

WAS THAT THING BLINKING BEFORE?
ZERO TO MAYFELD. ZERO TO MAYFELD.
WHAT?
I'VE DETECTED A NEW REPUBLIC DISTRESS SIGNAL HOMING IN ON YOUR LOCATION. YOU HAVE APPROXIMATELY TWENTY MINUTES.
GO, GO, GO!
SMASH!
Z, OPEN IT UP!
YOU HAVE FIFTEEN MINUTES REMAINING.
QIN.
FUNNY, THE MAN WHO LEFT ME BEHIND IS NOW MY SAVIOR.

THUNK!
BROTHER!
SISTER!
ATTACK'S ON THE WAY. HE'S ALREADY DEAD MEAT. LET'S GO!
SLAM!
ZERO TO MAYFELD, YOU HAVE A POTENTIAL PROBLEM.
HE HAS ESCAPED.

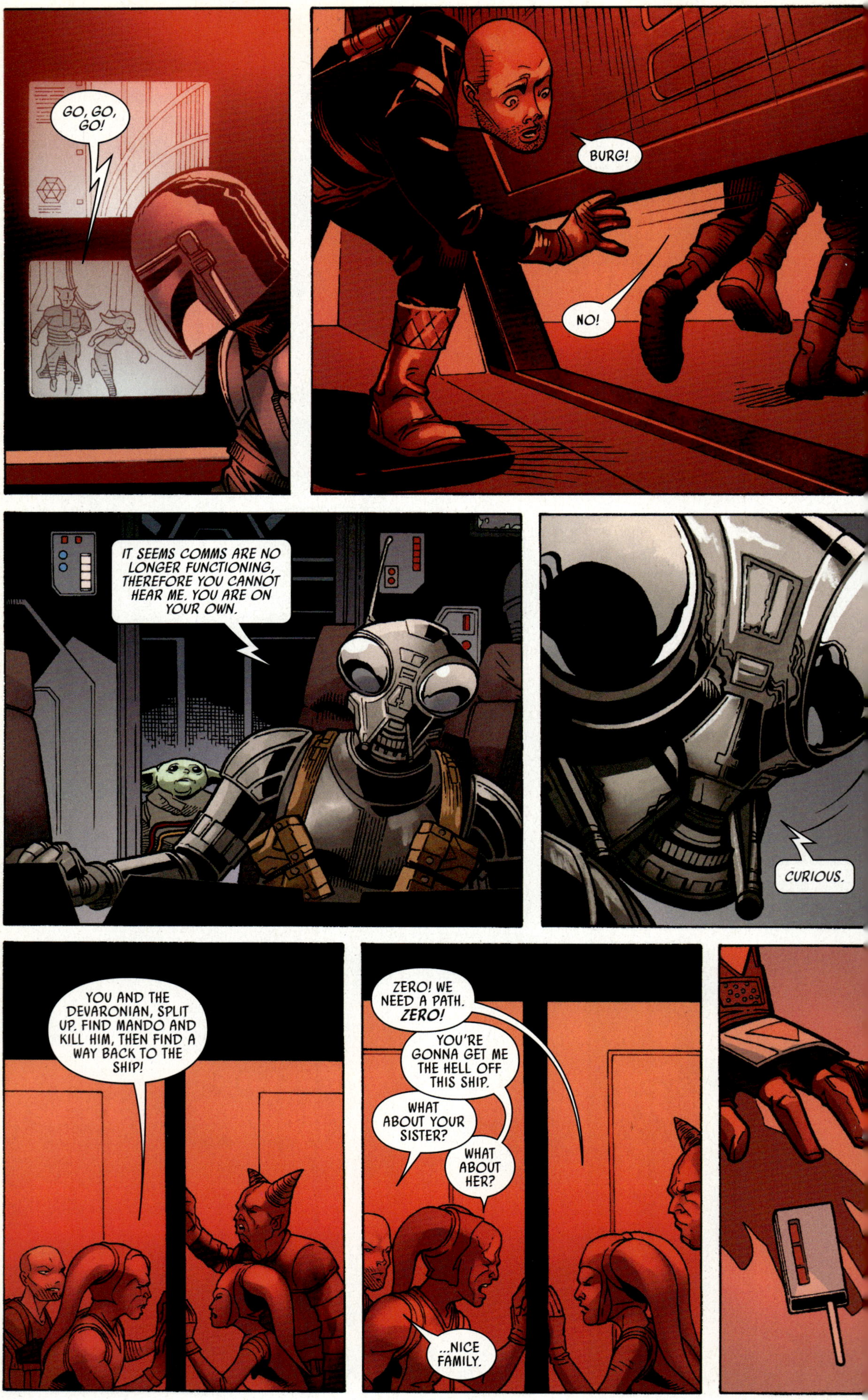
GO, GO, GO!
BURG!
NO!
IT SEEMS COMMS ARE NO LONGER FUNCTIONING, THEREFORE YOU CANNOT HEAR ME. YOU ARE ON YOUR OWN.
CURIOUS.
YOU AND THE DEVARONIAN, SPLIT UP. FIND MANDO AND KILL HIM, THEN FIND A WAY BACK TO THE SHIP!
ZERO! WE NEED A PATH. ZERO!
YOU'RE GONNA GET ME THE HELL OFF THIS SHIP.
WHAT ABOUT YOUR SISTER?
WHAT ABOUT HER?
...NICE FAMILY.

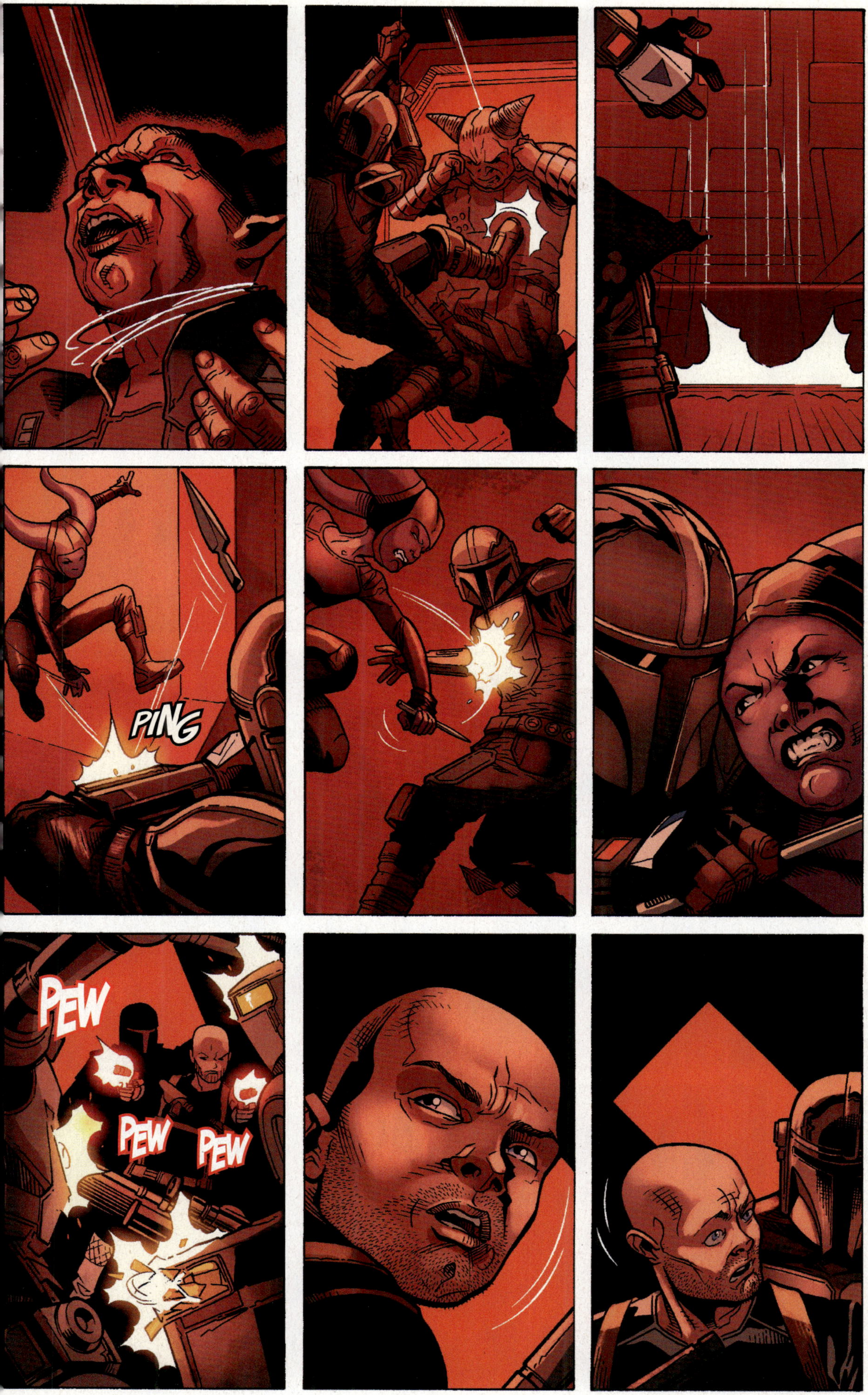
PING
PEW
PEW
PEW

QIN.
YOU KILLED THE OTHERS.
THEY GOT WHAT THEY DESERVED.
YOU KILL ME, YOU DON'T GET YOUR MONEY. WHATEVER RAN PROMISED, I'LL MAKE SURE YOU GET IT AND MORE. COME ON, MANDO. BE REASONABLE.
YOU WERE HIRED TO DO A JOB, RIGHT?
SO DO IT. ISN'T THAT YOUR CODE?
AREN'T YOU A MAN OF HONOR?

PEWSSH
VREEEEEEOOOM

WHERE ARE THE OTHERS?
NO QUESTIONS ASKED. THAT'S THE POLICY, RIGHT?
YEP, THAT *IS* THE POLICY.
I DID THE JOB.
YEAH, YOU DID.
JUST LIKE THE *GOOD OLD* DAYS.
YEAH, JUST LIKE THE GOOD OLD DAYS.

KILL HIM.
BEEPBEEPBEEPBEEP
BEEPBEEPBEEPBEEP
WHAT'S THIS?
THAT BASTARD.

I GOT A CLEAR SIGNAL ON THE TRACKING BEACON. LOOKS LIKE THEY'RE LAUNCHING A GUNSHIP.
COPY. GOIN' IN.
BOOM!
BOOM!
I TOLD YOU THAT WAS A BAD IDEA.

CHAPTER 7: THE RECKONING

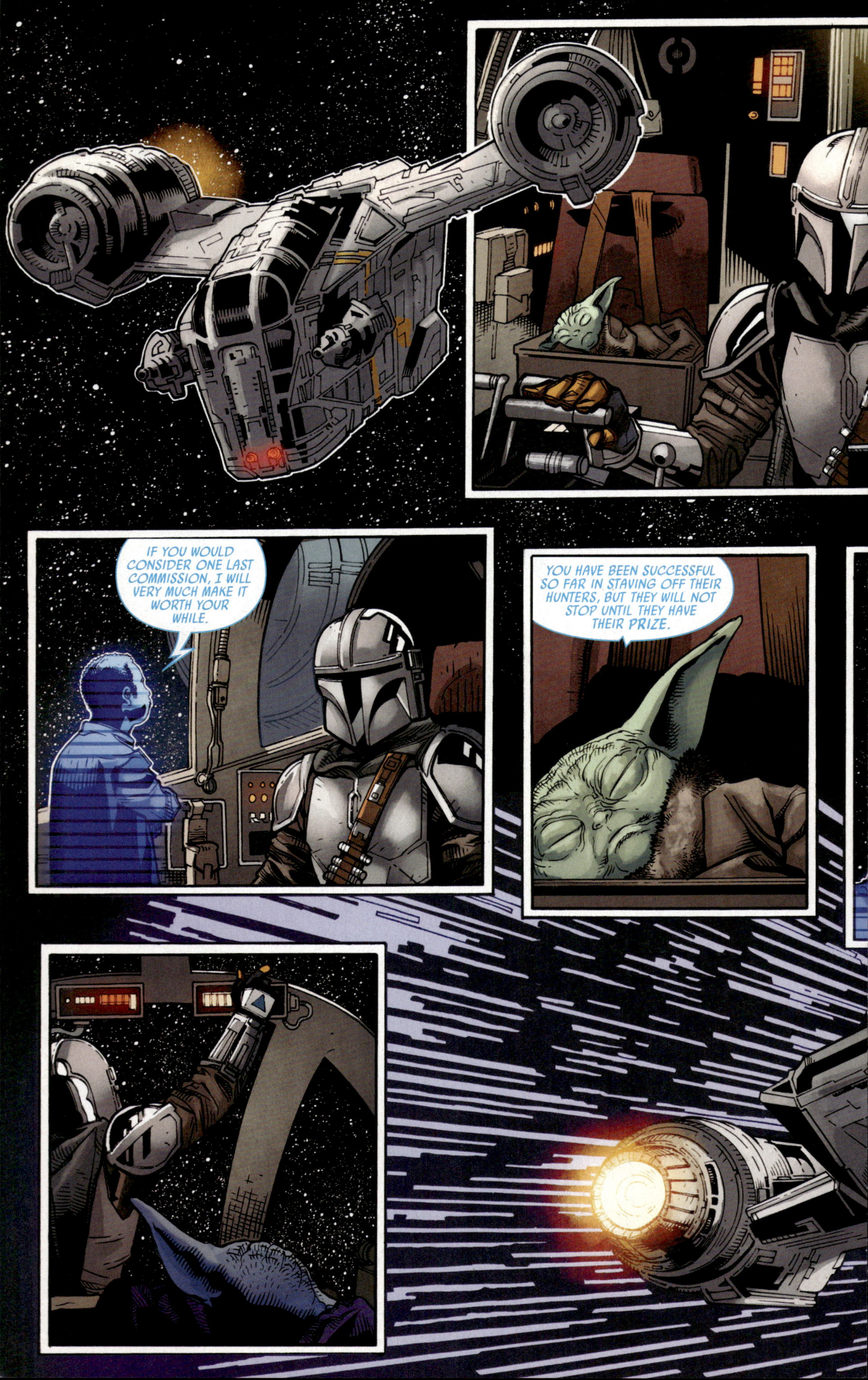
IF YOU WOULD CONSIDER ONE LAST COMMISSION, I WILL VERY MUCH MAKE IT WORTH YOUR WHILE.
YOU HAVE BEEN SUCCESSFUL SO FAR IN STAVING OFF THEIR HUNTERS, BUT THEY WILL NOT STOP UNTIL THEY HAVE THEIR PRIZE.

MY FRIEND, IF YOU ARE RECEIVING THIS TRANSMISSION, THAT MEANS YOU ARE ALIVE. YOU MIGHT BE SURPRISED TO HEAR THIS, BUT I AM ALIVE TOO.
I GUESS WE CAN CALL IT EVEN.
A LOT HAS HAPPENED SINCE WE LAST SAW EACH OTHER. THE MAN WHO HIRED YOU IS STILL HERE, AND HIS RANKS OF EX-IMPERIAL GUARDS HAVE GROWN.
THEY HAVE IMPOSED DESPOTIC RULE OVER MY CITY, WHICH HAS IMPEDED THE LIVELIHOOD OF THE GUILD. WE CONSIDER HIM AN ENEMY, BUT WE CANNOT GET CLOSE ENOUGH TO TAKE HIM OUT.
SO HERE IS MY PROPOSITION. RETURN TO NEVARRO. BRING THE CHILD AS BAIT. I WILL ARRANGE AN EXCHANGE AND PROVIDE LOYAL GUILD MEMBERS AS PROTECTION.
ONCE WE GET NEAR THE CLIENT, YOU KILL HIM, AND WE BOTH GET WHAT WE WANT.
IF YOU SUCCEED, YOU KEEP THE CHILD AND I WILL HAVE YOUR NAME CLEARED WITH THE GUILD.
FOR A MAN OF HONOR SHOULD NOT BE FORCED TO LIVE IN EXILE.
I AWAIT YOUR ARRIVAL WITH OPTIMISM.

CRACK!
CLACK!

KSSZZZ
HUAH!
AARRH!
PAY UP, MUDSCUFFERS!
LOOKING FOR SOME WORK?

IT SEEMS LIKE A STRAIGHTFORWARD OPERATION. THEY'RE PROVIDING THE PLAN AND FIREPOWER. I'M THE SNARE.
WITH THE KID?
THAT'S WHY I'M COMING TO YOU.
I DON'T KNOW, I'VE BEEN ADVISED TO LAY LOW. IF ANYBODY RUNS MY CHAIN CODE, I'LL ROT IN A CELL FOR THE REST OF MY LIFE.
I THOUGHT YOU WERE A VETERAN.
I'VE BEEN A LOT OF THINGS SINCE. MOST OF THEM CARRY A LIFE SENTENCE. IF I SO MUCH AS BOOK PASSAGE ON A SHIP REGISTERED TO THE NEW REPUBLIC, I'M--
I HAVE A SHIP. I CAN BRING YOU THERE AND BACK WITH A HANDSOME REWARD. YOU CAN LIVE FREE OF WORRY.
I'M ALREADY FREE OF WORRY. AND I'M NOT IN THE MOOD TO PLAY SOLDIER ANYMORE. ESPECIALLY FIGHTING SOME LOCAL WARLORD.
HE'S NOT A LOCAL WARLORD. HE'S IMPERIAL.
I'M IN.

DOES YOUR CONTACT NEED TO VET ME?
DOESN'T KNOW YOU'RE COMING.
REALLY? THAT COULD BE A PROBLEM.
IT WON'T. BUT IF IT *IS*, THAT'S HIS PROBLEM.
HE ALL RIGHT UP THERE ALONE?
YEAH.
PICK ONE.
YOU TRUST THE CONTACT?
NOT PARTICULARLY. HE AND I HAD A RUN-IN LAST TIME I WAS THERE ON SOME GUILD BUSINESS.
SO THEN *WHY* ARE WE GOING?
I DON'T HAVE A CHOICE. YOU SAW WHAT HAPPENED ON *SORGAN*. THEY'LL KEEP SENDING HUNTERS. THE KID WILL NEVER BE SAFE UNTIL THE IMP IS *DEAD*.
AND YOU'RE OKAY WITH BRINGING HIM BACK THERE?
NOT *REALLY*. THAT'S WHY I'M BRINGING YOU.
BGGGGRRRTTTTT!

WE NEED SOMEONE TO WATCH THAT THING.
YEAH.
YOU GOT ANYONE YOU CAN TRUST?

WHOA! EASY. WHOA!
IT HASN'T **GROWN** MUCH.
I THINK IT MIGHT BE A STRAND-CAST.
I DON'T THINK IT WAS ENGINEERED. I'VE WORKED IN THE GENE FARMS. THIS ONE LOOKS EVOLVED. TOO UGLY.
THIS ONE, ON THE OTHER HAND, LOOKS LIKE SHE WAS FARMED IN THE ***CYTOCAVES*** OF ***NORA***.
THIS IS ***CARA DUNE***. SHE WAS A SHOCK TROOPER.
YOU WERE A DROPPER?
DID YOU SERVE?
ON THE OTHER SIDE, I'M AFRAID. BUT I'M PROUD TO SAY THAT I PAID OUT MY CLAN'S DEBT, AND NOW I SERVE NO ONE BUT MYSELF.
WOULD ANYONE CARE FOR SOME TEA?
PLEASE LOWER YOUR BLASTERS. HE WILL NOT HARM YOU.
THAT THING IS PROGRAMMED TO KILL THE BABY.
NOT ANYMORE.

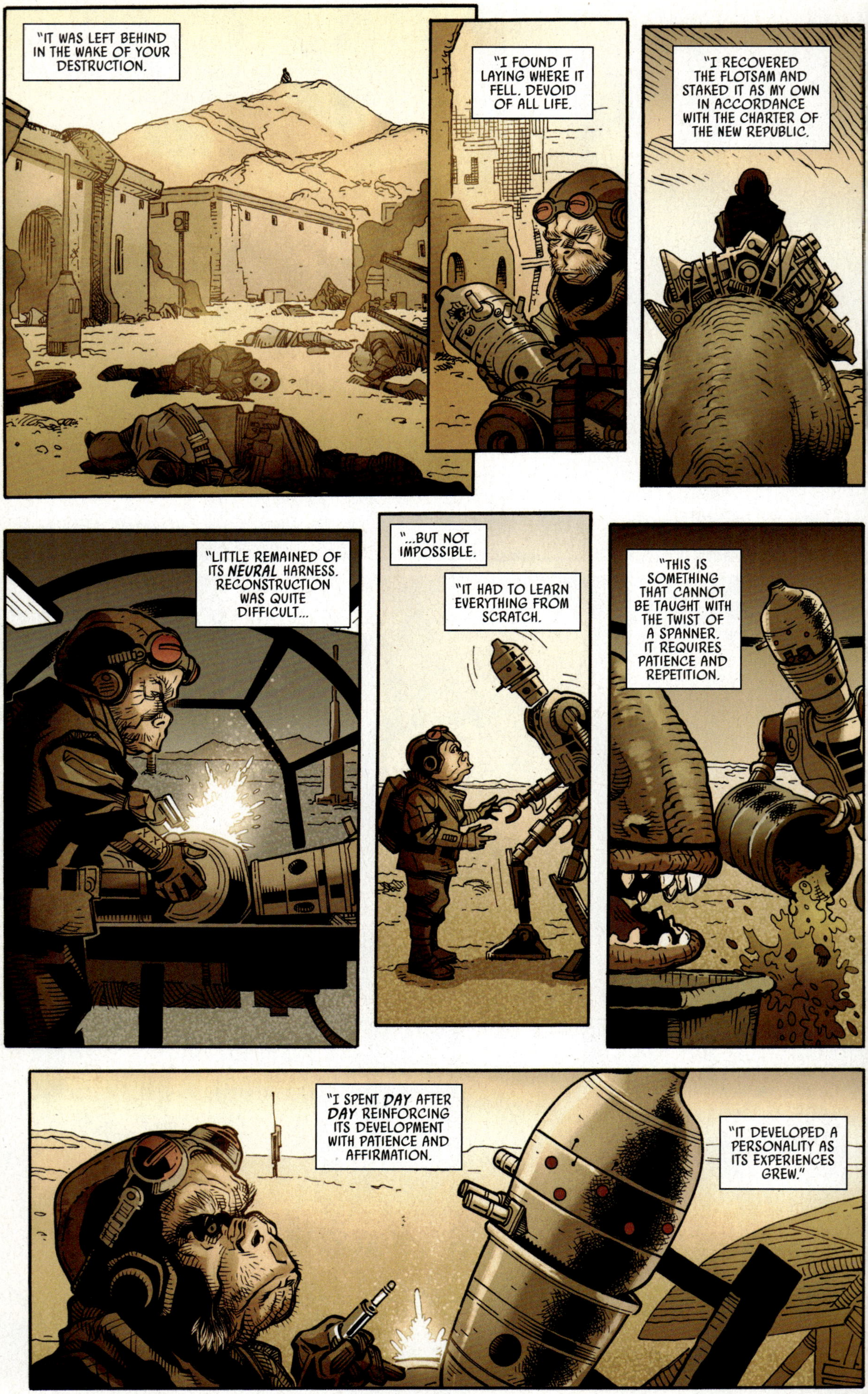
"IT WAS LEFT BEHIND IN THE WAKE OF YOUR DESTRUCTION.
"I FOUND IT LAYING WHERE IT FELL, DEVOID OF ALL LIFE.
"I RECOVERED THE FLOTSAM AND STAKED IT AS MY OWN IN ACCORDANCE WITH THE CHARTER OF THE NEW REPUBLIC.
"LITTLE REMAINED OF ITS *NEURAL* HARNESS. RECONSTRUCTION WAS QUITE DIFFICULT...
"...BUT NOT IMPOSSIBLE.
"IT HAD TO LEARN EVERYTHING FROM SCRATCH.
"THIS IS SOMETHING THAT CANNOT BE TAUGHT WITH THE TWIST OF A SPANNER. IT REQUIRES PATIENCE AND REPETITION.
"I SPENT *DAY* AFTER *DAY* REINFORCING ITS DEVELOPMENT WITH PATIENCE AND AFFIRMATION.
"IT DEVELOPED A PERSONALITY AS ITS EXPERIENCES GREW."

IS IT STILL A HUNTER?
NO, BUT IT WILL PROTECT.
TEA?
I'VE RUN INTO SOME *PROBLEMS*.
I WANNA HIRE YOUR SERVICES.
I FIGURED AS MUCH. WHY ELSE WOULD YOU RETURN?
I'M RETIRED FROM SERVICE.
I CAN PAY YOU HANDSOMELY, UGNAUGHT.
I HAVE A NAME. IT IS *KUIIL*.
I NEED SOMEONE TO PROTECT THE LITTLE ONE, *KUIIL*.
I'M NOT SUITED FOR SUCH WORK. I CAN REPROGRAM IG-11 FOR NURSING AND PROTOCOL...
NO. I DON'T WANT THAT DROID ANYWHERE NEAR HIM.
WHY ARE YOU SO DISTRUSTFUL OF DROIDS?
IT TRIED TO KILL HIM.

IT WAS PROGRAMMED TO DO SO. DROIDS ARE NOT GOOD OR BAD. THEY ARE NEUTRAL REFLECTIONS OF THOSE WHO IMPRINT THEM.
I'VE SEEN OTHERWISE.
DO YOU TRUST ME?
FROM WHAT I CAN TELL, YES.
THEN YOU WILL TRUST MY WORK.
IG-11 WILL JOIN ME. AND WE DO IT NOT FOR PAYMENT BUT TO PROTECT THE CHILD FROM IMPERIAL SLAVERY. NONE WILL BE FREE UNTIL THE OLD WAYS ARE GONE FOREVER.
OKAY.
AND THE BLURRGS WILL JOIN ME AS WELL.
THE BLURRGS?
I HAVE SPOKEN.

I GOT YOU, MANDO.
CARE TO DOUBLE THE BET?
UNGH.
NO! NO, STOP! WE'RE FRIENDS! CARA IS MY FRIEND!
HMM. VERY CURIOUS.
CURIOUS? IT ALMOST KILLED ME!
THE STORY YOU TOLD ME OF THE MUDHORN NOW MAKES MORE SENSE.
WHAT IS IT?
WHAT IT IS, I DON'T KNOW. BUT WHAT IT DOES, THIS... THIS I'VE HEARD RUMORS OF.
WHAT? WHEN YOU WORKED FOR THE EMPIRE?
WHEN I WAS SOLD TO THE EMPIRE, IN INDENTURED SERVITUDE.
YET SOMEHOW, YOU WALK FREE.
I BOUGHT MY FREEDOM THROUGH THE SKILL OF MY HANDS AND THE LABOR OF THREE OF YOUR HUMAN LIFETIMES.

DO NOT CAST DOUBT UPON THAT OF WHAT I AM NOR WHOM I SHALL SERVE.
TELL YOU WHAT. I COULD REALLY USE YOUR CRAFTWORK RIGHT NOW. CAN YOU PAD THIS CONTAINER SO THE CHILD CAN SLEEP BETTER?
I SHALL FABRICATE A BETTER ONE. THEN PERHAPS THIS DROPPER CAN SEE HOW ONE CAN WIN THEIR FREEDOM WITH THE SKILL OF ONE'S HANDS.
SO, WE'RE GOING TO NEVARRO.
HAVE YOU EVER BEEN?
NO. WE LOST A LOT OF OUR FORCES THERE. THE CITY'S DUG IN PRETTY DEEP. NO COVER WHEN YOU DROP IN.
IT STAYED IN EMPIRE CONTROL TILL THE END OF THE WAR.
THE WARLORD WE'RE TAKING OUT WAS AN IMPERIAL OFFICER.
WHAT STATION?
HARD TO TELL. NO INSIGNIA ANYMORE. I TOOK OUT THE SAFE HOUSE WHEN I SNATCHED THE KID. MORE IMPS HAVE REINFORCED SINCE.
THERE'S SOMETHING MORE GOING ON.
MAYBE. WE'LL FIND OUT MORE WHEN WE LAND.

I HAVE PREPARED SECOND MEAL. WOULD YOU CARE TO BE SERVED HERE OR BELOW?
I'M NOT HUNGRY.
UNDER NO CIRCUMSTANCES DOES THAT THING LEAVE THE SHIP.
YOU GOT A REAL THING FOR DROIDS, DON'T YOU?
I GOT A REAL THING FOR THAT DROID.
THE UGNAUGHT SAID HE REWIRED IT.
THAT DROID WAS DESIGNED TO KILL THINGS. I DON'T CARE HOW MUCH WIRING HE REPLACED. IT GOES AGAINST ITS NATURE.
WELL, IT SHOULDN'T BE A LONG JOB ANYWAY. WE TAKE OUT THE HEAD IMP, THE REST WILL RUN LIKE RATS.
SORRY FOR THE REMOTE RENDEZVOUS, MANDO, BUT THINGS HAVE GOTTEN COMPLICATED SINCE YOU WERE LAST HERE.
IT APPEARS THAT INTRODUCTIONS ARE IN ORDER.

IT SEEMS WE'VE BOTH PROVIDED A SECURITY DETAIL.
I RECOMMEND THE SHOCK TROOPER GUARDS THE SHIP, THESE LAVA FIELDS ARE LOUSY WITH JAWAS.
SHE'S COMING WITH ME.
BUT THE TOWN IS RUN BY EX-EMPIRE. IF A REBEL DROPPER IS WITH US, THEY'LL ALL GET THEIR HACKLES UP.
SHE'S COMING.
FINE. AT LEAST COVER YOUR TATTOO. NO NEED TO FLAUNT IT.
NOW, WHERE IS THE LITTLE ONE?
SO, THIS LITTLE BOGWING IS WHAT ALL THE FUSS WAS ABOUT. WHAT A PRECIOUS LITTLE CREATURE! I CAN SEE WHY YOU DIDN'T WANT TO HARM A HAIR ON ITS WRINKLED LITTLE HEAD.
WELL, I'M GLAD THIS MATTER WILL BE PUT TO REST ONCE AND FOR ALL.

"THE SUN DROPS FAST ON NEVARRO. WE CAN WALK FOR A SPELL, CAMP OUT AT THE RIVERBANK, THEN MAKE OUR WAY INTO TOWN AT FIRST LIGHT."
I GUESS THE LITTLE BUGGER'S A CARNIVORE. NEVER SEEN ANYTHING LIKE IT. THEY WERE READY TO PAY A KING'S RANSOM FOR THAT THING. MUST BE FOR SOME KIND OF HIGHFALUTIN MENAGERIE.
LET'S GO OVER THE PLAN AGAIN.
WE BOTH ENTER THE COMMON HOUSE. WE SHOW THE CLIENT THE BAIT. WE JOIN HIM AT THE TABLE. AND YOU KILL HIM.
TELL ME ABOUT HIS REINFORCEMENTS.
THEY'RE ALL EX-EMPIRE. AS SOON AS THEY LOSE THEIR PAYCHECK, POOF, THEY'LL ALL SCATTER.
AND WHAT IF THEY DON'T?
THEY WILL.

THAT'S NOT GOOD ENOUGH.
IF, FOR ARGUMENT'S SAKE, A FEW OF THEM DON'T REALIZE THAT I'M THEIR BEST PATH TO ALTERNATIVE EMPLOYMENT AND THEY ELECT TO REACT IMPULSIVELY, THEN THESE THREE FINE GUILD HUNTERS, ALONG WITH THAT BATTLE-HARDENED SHOCK TROOPER WILL CUT DOWN ANYONE WHO BUCKS.
HOW MANY WILL THERE BE?
NO MORE THAN FOUR. HE TRAVELS WITH, AT MOST, A FIRE TEAM. TRUST ME.
NOTHING CAN GO WRONG.
AGHH!

NO! LET GO OF HER! DROP HER NOW!
CHOOM CHOOM
CHOOM
FFFRRSHOOSH
PEW PEW PEW
PEW
PEW
PEW

HE'S HURT BADLY.
I'M FINE, I'M FI-- AGHHH!
HOLD STILL. THEY GOT YOU GOOD.
HOW BAD?
BAD. THE POISON'S SPREADING FAST.
SO THIS... THIS IS HOW IT HAPPENS.
DON'T BE SO DRAMATIC.
I NEED ANOTHER MEDPAC! GOT ANY OTHER MEDPACS? ANYONE?
I'M GUESSING THAT'S A "NO."
IT'S STILL SPREADING. THIS ISN'T WORKING.
GET THIS THING OUTTA HERE.
WAIT!
HE'S TRYING TO EAT ME!

YOU THINK THEY'RE HAVING SECOND THOUGHTS?
COULD BE. I NEED YOUR EYES.
I'M WATCHING.
I GUESS THIS IS IT.

PEW!
PEW!
THERE'S SOMETHING YOU SHOULD KNOW. THE PLAN WAS TO KILL YOU AND TAKE THE KID. BUT AFTER WHAT HAPPENED LAST NIGHT, I COULDN'T GO THROUGH WITH IT.
GO ON, YOU CAN GUN ME DOWN HERE AND NOW AND IT WOULDN'T VIOLATE THE CODE. BUT IF YOU DO, THIS CHILD WILL NEVER BE SAFE.
WE'LL TAKE OUR CHANCES.
THE IMPERIAL CLIENT IS OBSESSED WITH OBTAINING THIS ASSET. YOU TRIED TO RUN, BUT WHERE DID IT GET YOU?
THIS IS RIDICULOUS.
PERHAPS YOU SHOULD LET HIM SPEAK.
LISTEN. WE BOTH NEED THE CLIENT TO BE ELIMINATED. LET ME TAKE THE CHILD TO HIM AND THEN YOU TWO--
NO.
LET'S JUST KILL HIM AND GET OUTTA HERE.
HE'S RIGHT.
WHAT ARE YOU DOING?
AS LONG AS THE IMP LIVES, HE'LL SEND HUNTERS AFTER THE CHILD.

IT'S A TRAP.
BRING YOU?
BRING ME.
TELL HIM YOU CAPTURED ME. GET ME CLOSE TO HIM AND I'LL KILL HIM.
THAT'S A GOOD IDEA. GIVE ME YOUR BLASTER.
THIS IS INSANE!
IT'S THE ONLY WAY.
WELL, I'M COMING WITH YOU.
NO, NO, NO, THAT WOULD MAKE THEM SUSPICIOUS.
I DON'T CARE. I'M COMING.
TELL THEM SHE CAUGHT ME.
FINE. THEN SHE CAN BRING THE CHILD.
NO. THE KID GOES BACK IN THE SHIP.
I HAVE A PLAN.
BUT WITHOUT THE CHILD, NONE OF THIS WORKS!

KUIIL, RIDE BACK TO THE RAZOR CREST WITH THE CHILD AND SEAL YOURSELF IN. WHEN YOU'RE INSIDE, ENGAGE GROUND SECURITY PROTOCOLS. NOTHING ON THIS PLANET WILL BREACH THOSE DOORS.
I WILL KEEP THE CHILD SAFE.
CHAIN CODE?
I HAVE A GIFT FOR THE BOSS.
I'LL GIVE YOU TWENTY CREDITS FOR THE HELMET.
HA! NOT A CHANCE. THAT'S GOING ON MY WALL.
ON YOUR WALL?
GO WITH IT.
YOU SAID FOUR. THERE ARE MORE THAN FOUR TROOPERS.
FOUR GUARDING THE CLIENT. MANY MORE HERE IN TOWN. THINGS GOT REALLY HEATED ONCE MANDO CRASHED THE SAFE HOUSE.
SLIP HIM HIS BLASTER.
NOT YET.

HERE WE ARE.
YOU SEE? FOUR.
LOOK WHAT I BROUGHT YOU, AS PROMISED.
WHAT EXQUISITE CRAFTSMANSHIP. IT IS AMAZING HOW BEAUTIFUL BESKAR CAN BE WHEN FORGED BY ITS ANCESTRAL ARTISANS.
CAN I OFFER YOU A LIBATION TO CELEBRATE THE CLOSING OF OUR SHARED NARRATIVE?
I WOULD BE OBLIGED.
PLEASE SIT. IT IS A SHAME THAT YOUR PEOPLE SUFFERED SO. JUST AS IN THIS SITUATION, IT WAS ALL AVOIDABLE.

WHY DID MANDALORE RESIST OUR EXPANSION? THE EMPIRE IMPROVES EVERY SYSTEM IT TOUCHES. JUDGE BY ANY METRIC. SAFETY, PROSPERITY, TRADE, OPPORTUNITY, PEACE. COMPARE IMPERIAL RULE TO WHAT IS HAPPENING NOW.
LOOK OUTSIDE. IS THE WORLD MORE PEACEFUL SINCE THE REVOLUTION? I SEE NOTHING BUT DEATH AND CHAOS.
I WOULD LIKE TO SEE THE BABY.
UH...IT IS ASLEEP.
WE ALL WILL BE QUIET. OPEN THE PRAM.
DON'T THINK ME TO BE RUDE. I MUST TAKE THIS CALL.
GIVE ME THE BLASTER.
YOU GET ONE SHOT.

THIS IS BAD. YOU SAID FOUR.
WELL, THERE ARE MORE. WHAT CAN I TELL YOU?
YES, MOFF GIDEON?
HAVE THEY BROUGHT THE CHILD?
YES, THEY HAVE. CURRENTLY, IT IS SLEEPING.
YOU MAY WANT TO CHECK AGAIN.
CRASSSSMASH!

FOUR STORMTROOPERS?! THIS IS BAD.
KUIIL? ARE YOU BACK TO THE SHIP YET?
ARE YOU THERE? DO YOU COPY?
YES!
ARE YOU BACK TO THE SHIP YET?
NOT YET.
GET BACK TO THE SHIP AND BAIL. GET THE KID OUT OF HERE. WE'RE PINNED DOWN!

YOU HAVE SOMETHING I WANT.
WHO'S THIS GUY?
YOU MAY THINK YOU HAVE SOME IDEA OF WHAT YOU ARE IN POSSESSION OF, BUT YOU DO NOT.
KUIIL, ARE YOU BACK TO THE SHIP YET? THEY'RE ONTO US! KUIIL, COME IN!
IN A FEW MOMENTS, IT *WILL BE MINE.*

KUIIL, DO YOU COPY?! KUIIL!
IT MEANS MORE TO ME THAN YOU WILL EVER KNOW.
KUIIL, ARE YOU THERE?! COME IN, KUIIL!

KUIIL, ARE YOU THERE?! DO YOU COPY? KUIIL!!!

CHAPTER 8: **REDEMPTION**

SPEEDER BIKES HAVE ARRIVED AT THE CHECKPOINT WITH THE ASSET. AWAITING CONFIRMATION TO CONTINUE INTO TOWN.
BEHH?
KNOCK IT OFF!
THAT'S A GO TO PROCEED, BUT I ADVISE YOU TO DOUBLE-CHECK. THE MOFF JUST TOUCHED DOWN AND ALREADY TOOK OUT A SQUAD OF LOCAL TROOPERS.
DID HE JUST SAY THAT GIDEON KILLED HIS OWN MEN?
OH, WHO KNOWS? THESE GUYS LIKE TO LAY DOWN THE LAW WHEN THEY FIRST ARRIVE INTO TOWN.
BAHBAH.
PFFT!
I SAID, SHUT UP!
STOP THAT.

IDENTIFY YOURSELF!
I AM IG-11. I AM THIS CHILD'S NURSE DROID AND REQUIRE THAT YOU REMAND HIM TO ME IMMEDIATELY.
I'M SORRY, NURSE, BUT YOU'RE GONNA HAVE TO GET OUT OF HERE.
ARE YOU REFUSING MY REQUEST?
NO. I'M TELLING YOU TO GET OUT OF HE--
CRACK!
UUNGH!
GAH!
CRNCH!
THAT WAS UNPLEASANT. I'M SORRY YOU HAD TO SEE THAT.

THE MANDALORIANS HAVE A COVERT DOWN IN THE SEWERS. IF WE CAN GET DOWN THERE, THEY CAN HELP US ESCAPE. CHECKING FOR ACCESS POINTS.
THEY'RE SETTING UP AN E-WEB.
I FOUND THE SEWER VENT.
LET'S GET THE HELL OUT OF HERE.

IT'S ASSEMBLED! HOW LONG UNTIL THAT THING'S CLEARED?!
GET OUT OF THE WAY!
CHOOM
CHOOM
CHOOM
YOUR ASTUTE PANIC SUGGESTS THAT YOU UNDERSTAND YOUR SITUATION. I WOULD PREFER TO AVOID ANY FURTHER VIOLENCE AND ENCOURAGE A MOMENT OF CONSIDERATION.
MEMBERS OF MY ESCORT HAVE COMPLETED ASSEMBLY OF AN E-WEB HEAVY REPEATING BLASTER.
IF YOU ARE UNFAMILIAR WITH THIS WEAPON, I AM SURE THAT REPUBLICAN SHOCK TROOPER CARASYNTHIA DUNE OF ALDERAAN WILL ADVISE YOU THAT SHE HAS WITNESSED MANY OF HER RANKS VAPORIZED MID-DESCENT FACING THE PREDECESSOR OF THIS PARTICULAR MODEL.
OR PERHAPS THE DECOMMISSIONED MANDALORIAN HUNTER, DIN DJARIN, HAS HEARD THE SONGS OF THE SIEGE OF MANDALORE, WHEN GUNSHIPS OUTFITTED WITH SIMILAR ORDNANCE LAID WASTE TO FIELDS OF MANDALORIAN RECRUITS IN THE NIGHT OF A THOUSAND TEARS.
I ADVISE DISGRACED MAGISTRATE GREEF KARGA TO SEARCH THE WISDOM OF HIS YEARS AND URGE YOU TO LAY DOWN YOUR ARMS AND COME OUTSIDE.

WHAT DO YOU PROPOSE?
WHAT ASSURANCE DO YOU OFFER?
REASONABLE NEGOTIATION.
IF YOU'RE ASKING IF YOU CAN TRUST ME, YOU CANNOT. JUST AS YOU BETRAYED OUR BUSINESS ARRANGEMENT, I WOULD GLADLY BREAK ANY PROMISE AND WATCH YOU DIE AT MY HAND.
THE ASSURANCE I GIVE IS THIS: I WILL ACT IN MY OWN SELF-INTEREST, WHICH AT THIS TIME, INVOLVES YOUR COOPERATION AND BENEFIT.
I WILL GIVE YOU UNTIL NIGHTFALL, AND THEN I WILL HAVE THE E-WEB CANNON OPEN FIRE.

I SAY WE HEAR HIM OUT. AT LEAST OUT THERE, WE'VE GOT A SHOT.
THAT'S EASY FOR YOU TO SAY. I'M A REBEL SHOCK TROOPER. THEY'LL UPLOAD ME TO A MIND FLAYER. I'M SHOOTING MY WAY OUT OF HERE.
WHAT ABOUT YOU, MANDO?
I KNOW WHO HE IS. IT'S MOFF GIDEON.
NO. MOFF GIDEON WAS EXECUTED FOR WAR CRIMES.
IT'S HIM. HE KNEW MY NAME.
SO? WHAT DOES THAT PROVE?
I HAVEN'T HEARD THAT NAME SPOKEN SINCE I WAS A CHILD.
ON MANDALORE?
I WAS NOT BORN ON MANDALORE.
BUT YOU'RE A MANDALORIAN.
MANDALORIAN ISN'T A RACE.
IT'S A CREED.

PEWCRSSH!
"I WAS A *FOUNDLING*. THEY RAISED ME IN THE FIGHTING CORPS. I WAS TREATED AS ONE OF THEIR OWN."

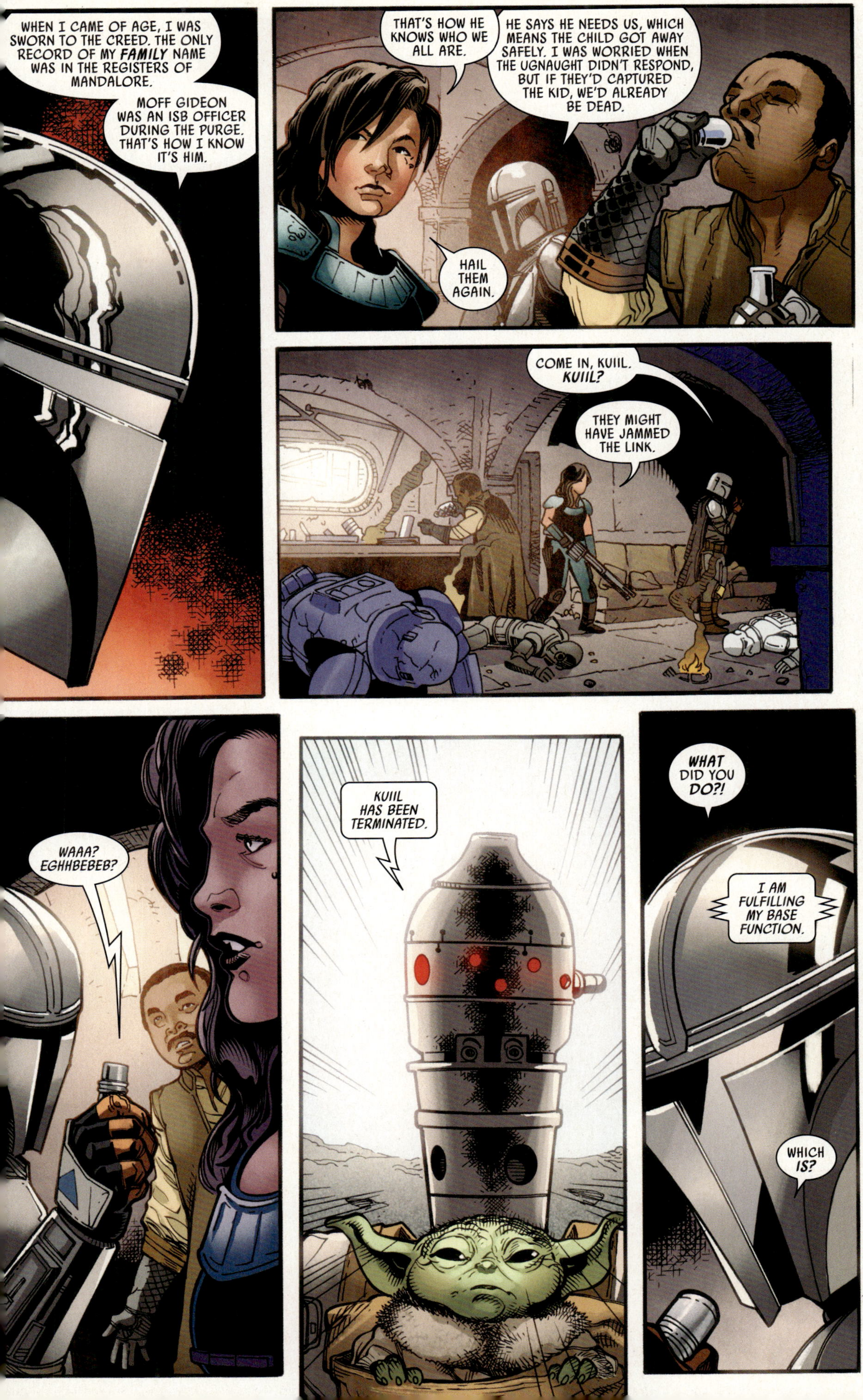
WHEN I CAME OF AGE, I WAS SWORN TO THE CREED. THE ONLY RECORD OF MY FAMILY NAME WAS IN THE REGISTERS OF MANDALORE.
MOFF GIDEON WAS AN ISB OFFICER DURING THE PURGE. THAT'S HOW I KNOW IT'S HIM.
THAT'S HOW HE KNOWS WHO WE ALL ARE.
HE SAYS HE NEEDS US, WHICH MEANS THE CHILD GOT AWAY SAFELY. I WAS WORRIED WHEN THE UGNAUGHT DIDN'T RESPOND, BUT IF THEY'D CAPTURED THE KID, WE'D ALREADY BE DEAD.
HAIL THEM AGAIN.
COME IN, KUIIL. KUIIL?
THEY MIGHT HAVE JAMMED THE LINK.
WAAA? EGHHBEBEB?
KUIIL HAS BEEN TERMINATED.
WHAT DID YOU DO?!
I AM FULFILLING MY BASE FUNCTION.
WHICH IS?

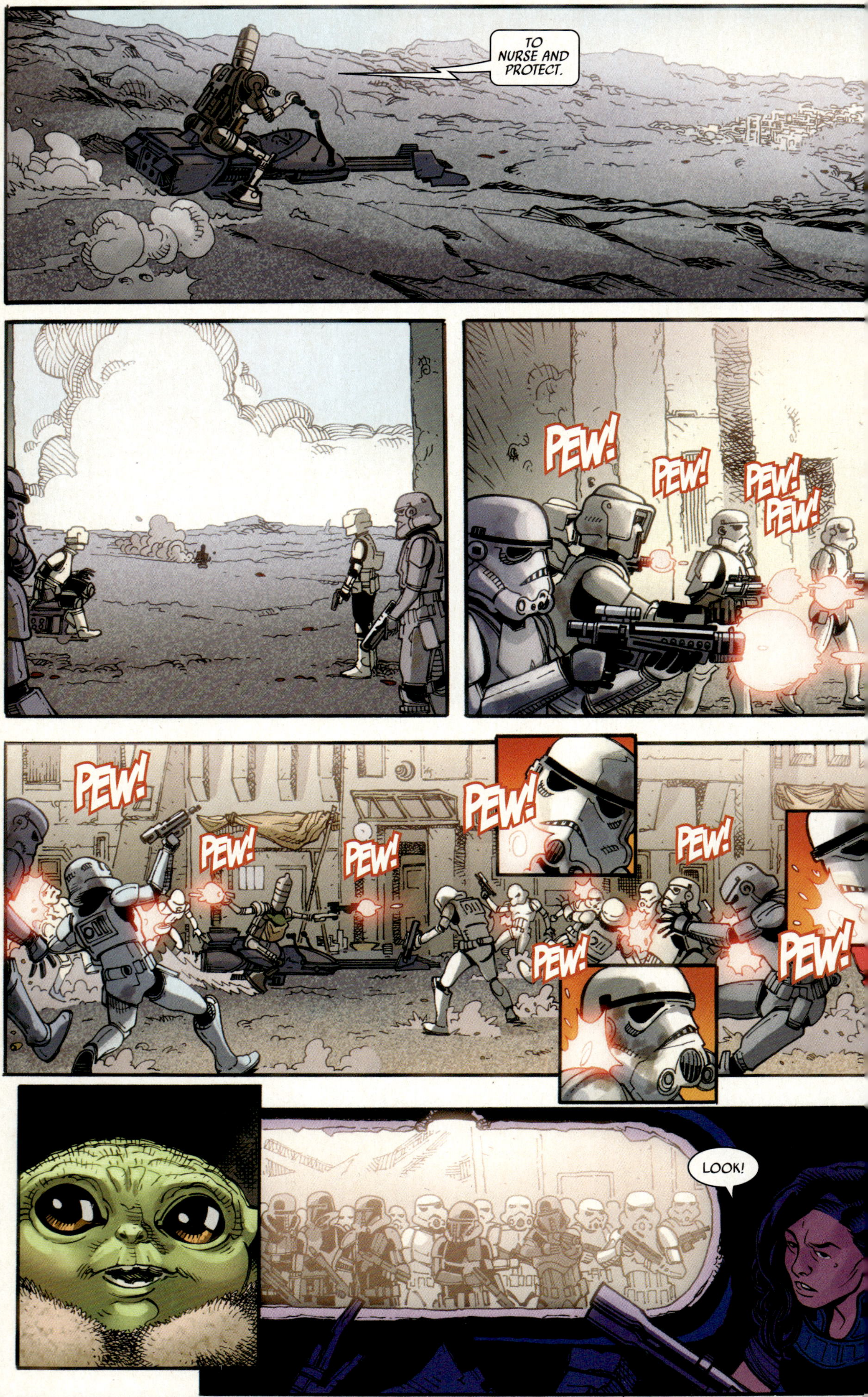
TO NURSE AND PROTECT.
PEW!
PEW!
PEW!
PEW!
PEW!
PEW!
PEW!
PEW!
PEW!
PEW!
PEW!
LOOK!

PEW!
PEW!
PEW!
PEW!
BOOM!
COVER ME!
PEW!
PEW!
PEW!
PEW!

PEW!
CHOOM CHOOM
CHOOM
CHOOM CHOOM
CHOOM
PEW!

PEW! PEW!
PEW!
PEW!
PEW!
BOOM!

BURN THEM OUT.
STAY WITH ME, BUDDY.
THIS IS OUR ONLY PATH OUT! CAN YOU CLEAR IT?
SSSZZZ
I'M NOT GONNA MAKE IT. GO.
YOU JUST GOT YOUR BELL RUNG. YOU'LL BE FINE.
LEAVE ME.
I'M GONNA NEED TO TAKE THIS THING OFF.
NO! YOU LEAVE ME. YOU MAKE SURE THE CHILD IS SAFE. HERE.

WHEN YOU GET TO THE MANDALORIAN COVERT, YOU SHOW THEM THAT. TELL THEM IT'S FROM DIN DJARIN. TELL THEM THE FOUNDLING WAS IN MY PROTECTION, AND THEY'LL HELP YOU.
FRRRSSH
YOU PROTECT THE CHILD. I CAN HOLD THEM BACK LONG ENOUGH FOR YOU TO ESCAPE. LET ME HAVE A WARRIOR'S DEATH.
I WON'T LEAVE YOU.
THIS IS THE WAY.

FRRRSSH
FRRRSSH
KRSINK
IT'S OPEN, LET'S GO!
GO.
ESCAPE AND PROTECT THIS CHILD. I WILL STAY WITH THE MANDALORIAN.

PROMISE ME YOU'LL BRING HIM.
YOU HAVE MY WORD.
I NEED TO REMOVE YOUR HELMET IF I AM TO SAVE YOU.
TRY IT AND I'LL KILL YOU. IT IS FORBIDDEN. NO LIVING THING HAS SEEN ME WITHOUT MY HELMET SINCE I SWORE THE CREED.
I AM NOT A LIVING THING.

THIS IS A BACTA SPRAY. IT WILL HEAL YOU IN A MATTER OF HOURS. YOU HAVE SUFFERED DAMAGE TO YOUR CENTRAL PROCESSING UNIT.
SSSSS
YOU MEAN MY BRAIN?
THAT WAS A JOKE. IT IS MEANT TO PUT YOU AT EASE.
I GOT YOU.
TURN HERE.

WE SHOULD GO.
YOU GO. TAKE THE SHIP. I CAN'T LEAVE IT THIS WAY.
DID YOU KNOW ABOUT THIS? IS THIS THE WORK OF YOUR BOUNTY HUNTERS?
IT WAS NOT HIS FAULT.
WE REVEALED OURSELVES. WE KNEW WHAT COULD HAPPEN IF WE LEFT THE COVERT. THE IMPERIALS ARRIVED SHORTLY THEREAFTER.
SHOW ME THE ONE WHOSE SAFETY DEEMED SUCH DESTRUCTION.
THIS IS THE ONE THAT YOU HUNTED, THEN SAVED?
YES. THE ONE THAT SAVED ME AS WELL.
FROM THE MUDHORN?
YES.

ITS SPECIES CAN MOVE OBJECTS WITH ITS MIND.
I KNOW OF SUCH THINGS. THE SONGS OF EONS PAST TELL OF BATTLES BETWEEN MANDALORE THE GREAT AND AN ORDER OF SORCERERS CALLED JEDI THAT FOUGHT WITH SUCH POWERS.
IT IS AN ENEMY?
WHAT IS IT?
NO. ITS KIND WERE ENEMIES, BUT THIS INDIVIDUAL IS NOT.
IT IS A FOUNDLING. BY CREED, IT IS IN YOUR CARE. YOU MUST REUNITE IT WITH ITS OWN KIND.
YOU EXPECT ME TO SEARCH THE GALAXY FOR THE HOME OF THIS CREATURE AND DELIVER IT TO A RACE OF ENEMY SORCERERS?
THIS IS THE WAY.
THESE TUNNELS WILL BE LOUSY WITH IMPS IN A MATTER OF MINUTES.
IF YOU FOLLOW THE DESCENDING TUNNEL, IT WILL LEAD YOU TO THE UNDERGROUND RIVER. IT FLOWS DOWNSTREAM TOWARD THE LAVA FLATS.
I'M STAYING. I NEED TO HELP HER, AND I NEED TO HEAL.
YOU MUST GO. A FOUNDLING IS IN YOUR CARE. BY CREED, UNTIL IT IS OF AGE OR REUNITED WITH ITS OWN KIND, YOU ARE AS ITS FATHER. THIS IS THE WAY.
YOU HAVE EARNED YOUR SIGNET. YOU ARE A CLAN OF TWO.
THANK YOU. I WILL WEAR THIS WITH HONOR.

I HAVE ONE MORE GIFT FOR YOUR JOURNEY. HAVE YOU TRAINED IN THE RISING PHOENIX?
WHEN I WAS A BOY. YES.
THEN THIS WILL MAKE YOU COMPLETE. WHEN YOU HAVE HEALED, YOU WILL BEGIN YOUR DRILLS. UNTIL YOU KNOW IT, IT WILL NOT LISTEN TO YOUR COMMANDS.
"MORE WILL COME. YOU MUST GO."
"COME WITH US."
"MY PLACE IS HERE. NOW GO! DOWN TO THE RIVER AND ACROSS THE PLAINS.
"BE SAFE ON YOUR JOURNEY."
"THANK YOU."
HEY, MANDO.
WHERE ARE THEY?
I SAID, WHERE ARE THEY?!
CRACK!

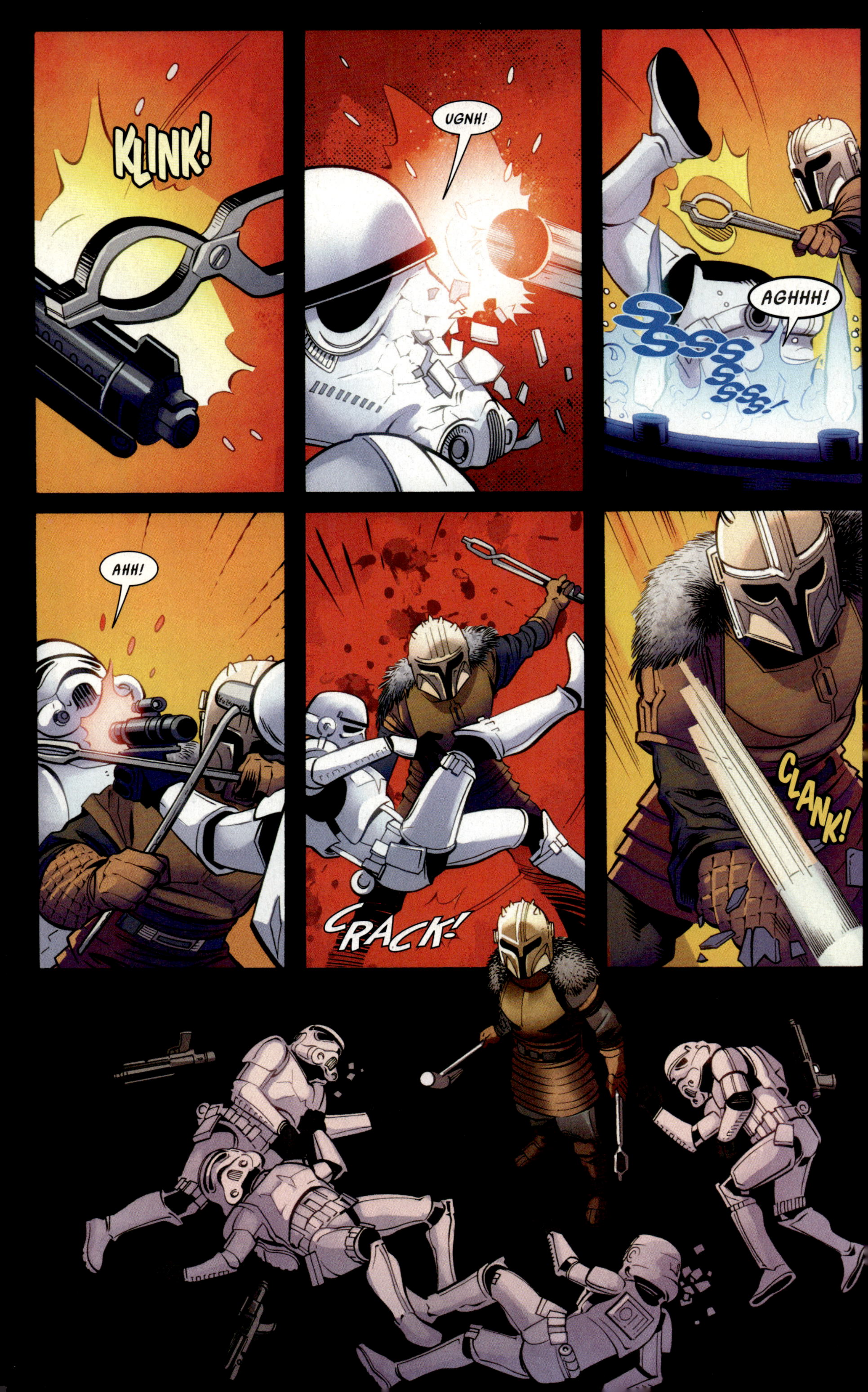
KLINK!
UGNH!
AGHHH!
SSSSSSSS!
AHH!
CRACK!
CLANK!

THIS IS THE LAVA RIVER.
THE FERRY DROID IS FRIED.
YEAH, BUT IF WE PUSH THE BOAT OUT, WE CAN GET IT TO FLOAT DOWNSTREAM. COME ON.
WATCH YOUR FEET. IT'S MOLTEN LAVA.
NO KIDDING.
BEEP BOOP BLIP
I BELIEVE HE IS ASKING WHERE WE WOULD LIKE TO GO.
DOWN-RIVER. TO THE LAVA FLAT.
BLIP BLIP BOOP
THAT'S IT! WE'RE FREE!

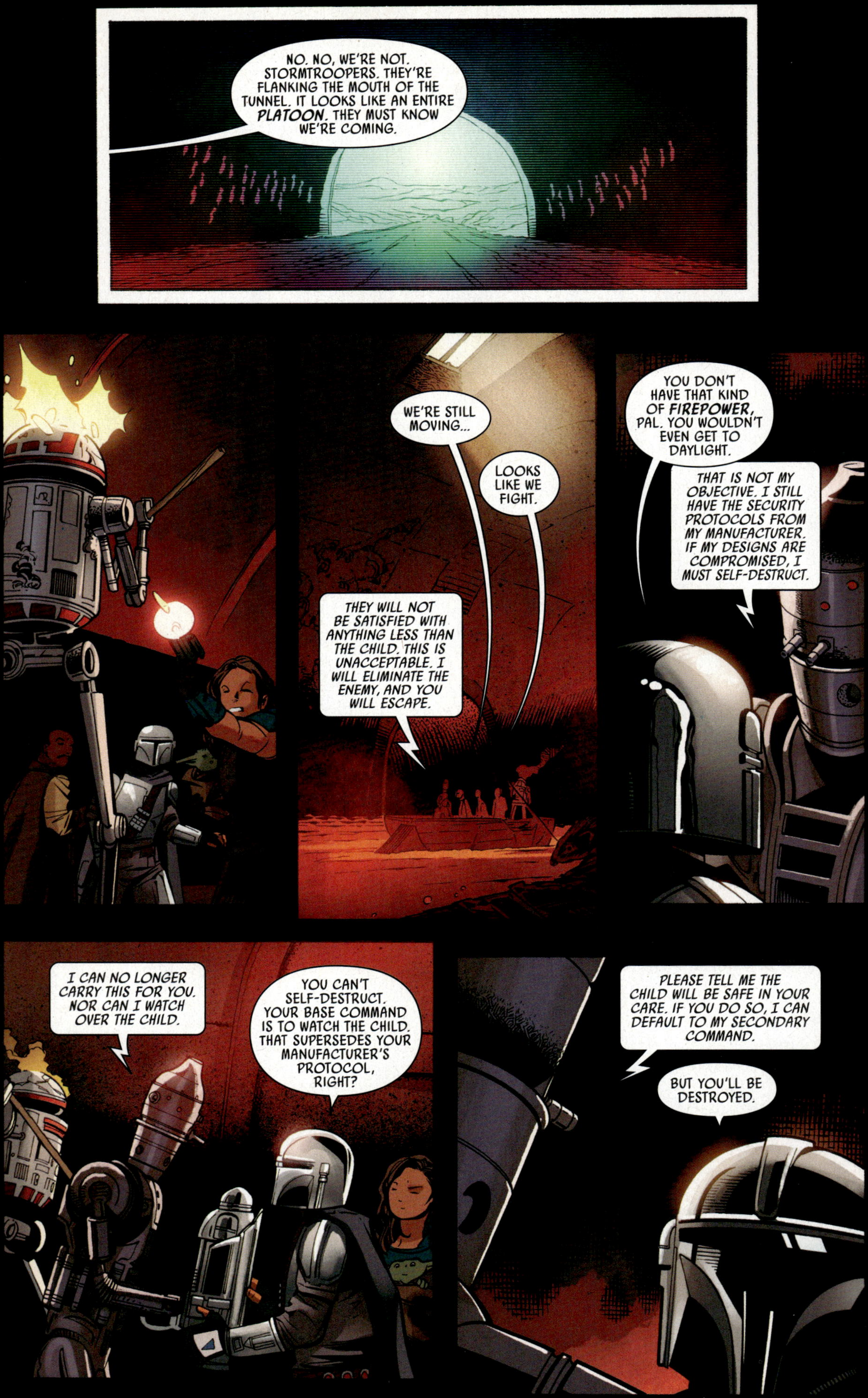

NO. NO, WE'RE NOT. STORMTROOPERS. THEY'RE FLANKING THE MOUTH OF THE TUNNEL. IT LOOKS LIKE AN ENTIRE *PLATOON*. THEY MUST KNOW WE'RE COMING.
WE'RE STILL MOVING...
LOOKS LIKE WE FIGHT.
THEY WILL NOT BE SATISFIED WITH ANYTHING LESS THAN THE CHILD. THIS IS UNACCEPTABLE. I WILL ELIMINATE THE ENEMY, AND YOU WILL ESCAPE.
YOU DON'T HAVE THAT KIND OF *FIREPOWER*, PAL. YOU WOULDN'T EVEN GET TO DAYLIGHT.
THAT IS NOT MY OBJECTIVE. I STILL HAVE THE SECURITY PROTOCOLS FROM MY MANUFACTURER. IF MY DESIGNS ARE COMPROMISED, I MUST SELF-DESTRUCT.
I CAN NO LONGER CARRY THIS FOR YOU. NOR CAN I WATCH OVER THE CHILD.
YOU CAN'T SELF-DESTRUCT. YOUR BASE COMMAND IS TO WATCH THE CHILD. THAT SUPERSEDES YOUR MANUFACTURER'S PROTOCOL, RIGHT?
PLEASE TELL ME THE CHILD WILL BE SAFE IN YOUR CARE. IF YOU DO SO, I CAN DEFAULT TO MY SECONDARY COMMAND.
BUT YOU'LL BE DESTROYED.

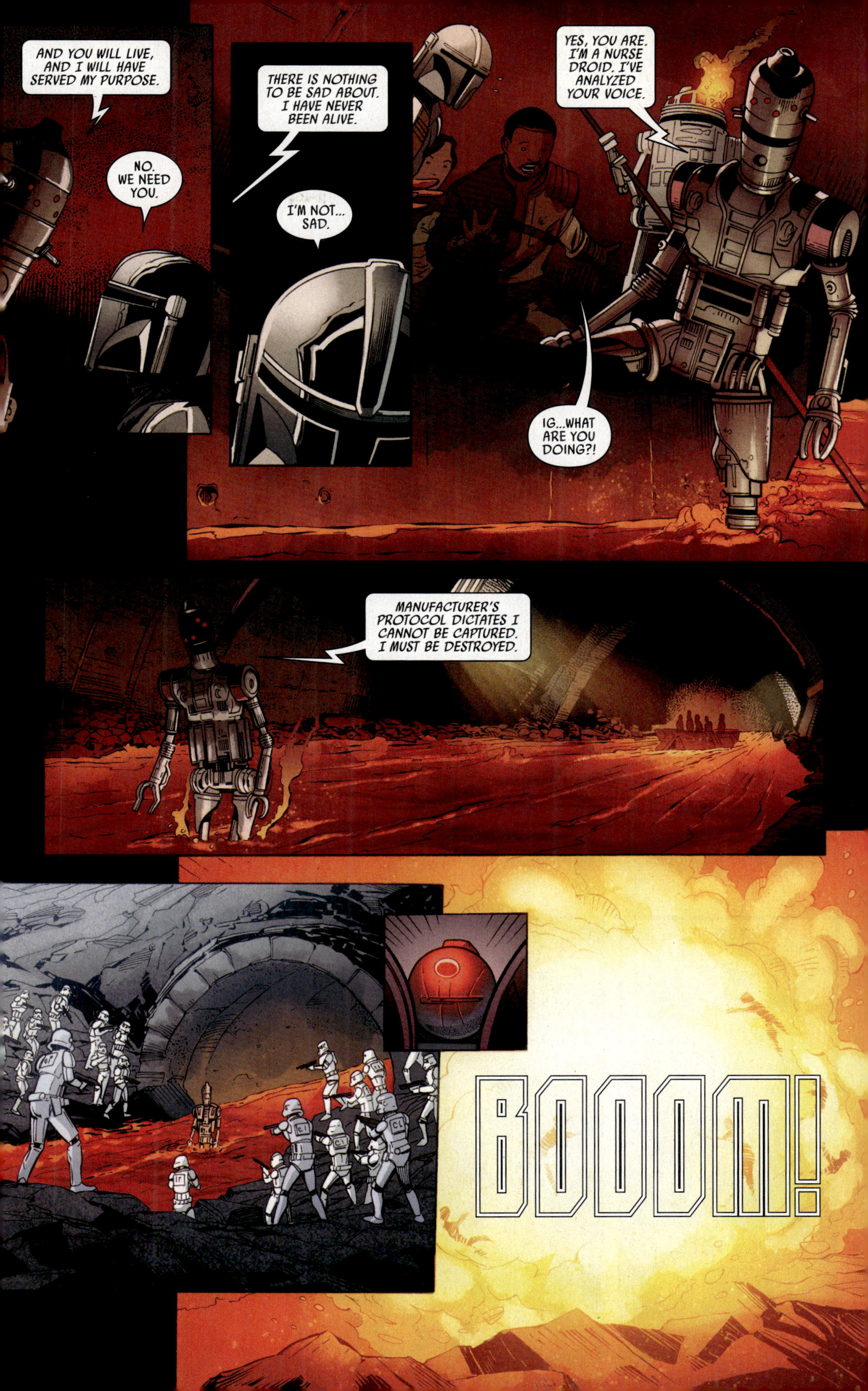
AND YOU WILL LIVE, AND I WILL HAVE SERVED MY PURPOSE.
NO. WE NEED YOU.
THERE IS NOTHING TO BE SAD ABOUT. I HAVE NEVER BEEN ALIVE.
I'M NOT... SAD.
YES, YOU ARE. I'M A NURSE DROID. I'VE ANALYZED YOUR VOICE.
IG...WHAT ARE YOU DOING?!
MANUFACTURER'S PROTOCOL DICTATES I CANNOT BE CAPTURED. I MUST BE DESTROYED.
BOOOM!

MOFF GIDEON!
PEW! PEW!
PEW! PEW!
OUR BLASTERS ARE USELESS AGAINST HIM.
COME ON, BABY, DO THE MAGIC-HAND THING!
I'M OUT OF IDEAS.
I'M NOT.

CRSH!

NO!
BOOM!
THAT WAS IMPRESSIVE, MANDO. VERY IMPRESSIVE. IT LOOKS LIKE YOUR GUILD RATES HAVE JUST GONE UP.
ANY MORE STORMTROOPERS?
I THINK WE CLEANED UP THE TOWN. I'M THINKING OF STAYING AROUND JUST TO BE SURE.
YOU'RE STAYING HERE?
AS A BOUNTY HUNTER HIVE?
WELL, WHY NOT? NEVARRO IS A VERY FINE PLANET! AND NOW THAT THE SCUM AND VILLAINY HAVE BEEN WASHED AWAY, IT'S VERY RESPECTABLE AGAIN.
SOME OF MY FAVORITE PEOPLE ARE BOUNTY HUNTERS!
AND PERHAPS THIS SPECIMEN OF SOLDIER MIGHT CONSIDER JOINING OUR RANKS.
YEAH, I'VE GOT SOME... CLERICAL CONCERNS REGARDING MY CHAIN CODE.
AND IF YOU WOULD AGREE TO BECOME MY ENFORCER, CLERICAL CONCERNS WOULD BE THE LEAST OF YOUR WORRIES.

BUT YOU, MY FRIEND, YOU WILL BE WELCOME BACK INTO THE GUILD WITH OPEN ARMS. SO GO OFF, ENJOY YOURSELF. AND WHEN YOU'RE READY TO RETURN, YOU WILL HAVE THE PICK OF ALL QUARRIES.
I'M AFRAID I HAVE MORE PRESSING MATTERS AT HAND.
TAKE CARE OF THIS LITTLE ONE.
OR MAYBE IT'LL TAKE CARE OF YOU.
WHAT DO YOU GOT THERE?
I DIDN'T THINK I'D SEE THIS AGAIN. WHY DON'T YOU HANG ONTO THAT?

KKKRRRGGGGT!
AGHHH!
The end....for now.

#5 Concept Art Variant by
CHRISTIAN ALZMANN

#6 Concept Art Variant by
BRIAN MATYAS

#7 Concept Art Variant by
CHRISTIAN ALZMANN

#8 Concept Art Variant by
RYAN CHURCH

#5 Variant by
E.M. GIST

#5 Variant by
RACHAEL STOTT

#6 Variant by
RICKIE YAGAWA & **JORDIE BELLAIRE**

#6 Variant by
RAHZZAH

#7 Variant by
TAURIN CLARKE

#7 Variant by
JOSHUA "SWAY" SWABY

#8 Variant by
MAHMUD ASRAR & MATTHEW WILSON

#8 Variant by
TERRY DODSON & RACHEL DODSON

#8 Black History Month Variant by
MATEUS MANHANINI

VADER DEMONSTRATES WHAT HAPPENS TO THOSE WHO WOULD CHALLENGE THE EMPIRE!
ALSO AVAILABLE:
PAK • IENCO • MENON
MARVEL
STAR WARS
DARTH VADER
DARK HEART OF THE SITH
STAR WARS: DARTH VADER BY GREG PAK VOL. 1: DARK HEART OF THE SITH TPB
978-1302920814
PAK • IENCO • MENON
MARVEL
STAR WARS
DARTH VADER
INTO THE FIRE
STAR WARS: DARTH VADER BY GREG PAK VOL. 2: INTO THE FIRE TPB
978-1302920821
GREG PAK
WEAVES A DARK TALE OF VIOLENCE AND VENGEANCE IN THE WAKE OF *THE EMPIRE STRIKES BACK*.
PAK • KIRK • VILANOVA • IENCO
MARVEL
STAR WARS
DARTH VADER
CRIMSON REIGN
STAR WARS: DARTH VADER BY GREG PAK VOL. 4 - CRIMSON REIGN TPB
978-1302926236
STAR WARS
WAR OF THE BOUNTY HUNTERS
DARTH VADER
PAK
VILANOVA
IENCO
MARVEL
STAR WARS: DARTH VADER BY GREG PAK VOL. 3: WAR OF THE BOUNTY HUNTERS TPB
978-1302926229
ON SALE NOW
IN PRINT AND DIGITAL WHEREVER BOOKS ARE SOLD.
TO FIND A COMIC SHOP NEAR YOU, VISIT COMICSHOPLOCATOR.COM.
MARVEL
© 2022 MARVEL

THE REBELLION STRIKES BACK.
SOULE • SAIZ • PRIANTO
MARVEL
STAR WARS
THE DESTINY PATH
ON SALE NOW
IN PRINT AND DIGITAL WHEREVER BOOKS ARE SOLD.
TO FIND A COMIC SHOP NEAR YOU, VISIT COMICSHOPLOCATOR.COM.
STAR WARS VOL. 1: THE DESTINY PATH TPB
978-1302920784
© 2022 MARVEL

READ THE REST OF THE STORY IN THIS ACCLAIMED GRAPHIC NOVEL!

ALYSSA **WONG**

MARIKA **CRESTA**

STAR WARS: DOCTOR APHRA VOL. 1: FORTUNE AND FATE TPB

978-1302923044

"FEATURES CHARACTERS WE LOVE (BOTH NEW AND OLD), CREATIVE WRITING TECHNIQUES, AND BRILLIANT ARTWORK"

– MONKEYS FIGHTING ROBOTS

"EXCELLENT WRITING FROM ALYSSA WONG AND STRONG ARTWORK FROM MARIKA CRESTA"

– IMPULSE GAMER

"DR. APHRA IS A GREAT NEW CHARACTER AND I WOULD LIKE TO SEE MORE OF HER"

– GRAPHIC POLICY

ON SALE NOW

AVAILABLE IN PRINT AND DIGITAL WHEREVER BOOKS ARE SOLD.
TO FIND A COMIC SHOP NEAR YOU, VISIT COMICSHOPLOCATOR.COM.

MARVEL